For God, Gold and Glory

D1732808

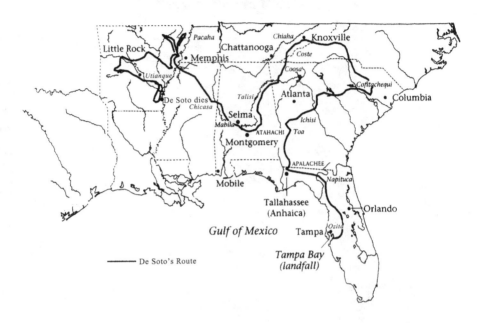

Little Rock
Pacaha
Chattanooga
Chiaha
Knoxville
Memphis
Coste
Coosa
Utiangue
De Soto dies
Talisi
Atlanta
Cofitachequi
Chicasa
Columbia
Selma
Ichisi
Mabila
ATAHACHI
Toa
Montgomery
APALACHEE
Napituca
Mobile
Tallahassee
(Anhaica)
Orlando
Gulf of Mexico
Tampa
Ozita

Tampa Bay
(landfall)

———— De Soto's Route

Hernando de Soto's Travels in the American South

Courtesy of David Ewing Duncan and Charles Hudson

For God, Gold and Glory

De Soto's Journey to the Heart of *La Florida*

A novel

E. H. Haines

Pineapple Press, Inc.
Sarasota, Florida

Copyright © 2008 by E. H. Haines

All rights reserved. No part of this book may be reproduced in any form or by
any means, electronic or mechanical, including photocopying, recording, or
by any information storage and retrieval system, without permission in writing
from the publisher.

Inquiries should be addressed to:

Pineapple Press, Inc.
P.O. Box 3889
Sarasota, Florida 34230

www.pineapplepress.com

Library of Congress Cataloging-in-Publication Data

Haines, E. H.
  For God, gold and glory : De Soto's journey to the heart of la Florida / E.H.
Haines. -- 1st ed.
    p. cm.
  ISBN 978-1-56164-428-5 (hardback : alk. paper)
  1. Soto, Hernando de, ca. 1500-1542--Fiction. 2. Explorers--Spain--Fiction.
3. Explorers--America--Fiction. 4. Florida--Discovery and exploration--
Spanish--Fiction. 5. Florida--History--To 1565--Fiction. I. Title.
  PS3608.A5448G63 2008
  813'.6--dc22
                                    2008015154

First Edition
10 9 8 7 6 5 4 3 2 1

Design by Shé Heaton
Printed in the United States of America

To my wife, Gloria,
for her kind and loving patience

Prologue

I had not seen or heard from Arturo LaBelle for over thirty years, so I was surprised to receive a small manuscript from him, mailed from Mexico City. Arturo and I roomed at the same boarding house while in graduate school at the University of Florida, Gainesville.

Arturo was tall, handsome, and Mexican, of Spanish heritage. He was friendly, if at times aristocratic. His family had something to do with the oil business in Mexico. He mailed the manuscript to me because he knew I had published several books. Arturo had acquired the original manuscript at a family reunion several years before and finally had it translated and typed into English. It had been written by a distant relative of his in the late 1500s.

As it turned out, Arturo's relative was Rodrigo Ranjel, the private secretary of Hernando de Soto during his invasion of North America in 1539. In this work Ranjel, writing years later from his notes, looks back at his five years with de Soto. Ranjel's writing covers the period from when he first met de Soto until de Soto's death near the Mississippi River in 1542. Ranjel survived the ordeal and died a modestly wealthy man in Mexico City in 1568. I have filled in a few gaps and made some corrections to Ranjel's work based on what is known by historians today.

I took the manuscript to a friend, Dr. Charles Lens. Dr. Lens is an archaeologist and historian with the state of Florida. Charley was excited by this important new piece of Florida history, and he provided me with a mountain of background data to incorporate into the book for "a full and better understanding of the reader." However, it would be difficult to incorporate this information and data, most of which was not available to Ranjel, into what is a first-person narrative; further, it would bog down the telling of this adventure. Thus, I have chosen to place a few italicized comments from Charley's material at the end of each chapter. I hope this helps the reader better understand this tragic tale of the first invasion of what is now the southeastern United States.

E. H. Haines
Fort Myers, Florida

For God, Gold and Glory

Chapter 1

I am sharpening my sword for the last time. For some twenty years it has hung on the stones above the hearth gathering dust. I'm now an old man.

The grip feels familiar to my hand; the blade was crafted from the best Damascus steel, the mark of Toledo on the hilt. It is a thin, double blade, and was given to me by my father on my tenth birthday. My father was a good Catholic who fought during the Inquisition. I am proud, for this sword has never killed a Christian.

My oldest son, Basilio, sailed back to Seville years ago. He has asked that I write of *La Florida*. He believes that I am the only man still alive who was with the Governor during the entire *entrada*. Basilio is upset that many in Spain write of the Governor and *La Florida* without having known him or having set foot in that land. Those things do not disturb me; it is the nature of man.

I needed to hold my sword again, for it was with me the day I met the Governor, and it was with me five years later when we lowered his body into the cold, dark water.

I, Rodrigo Ranjel, first saw the Governor, Hernando de Soto, in Seville in the spring of 1536. I was part of the raucous crowd as he and his triumphant party embarked and, riding in decorated carts, were paraded through the streets to the great cathedral. There they gave thanks to God for their safe passage home. De Soto was Castile's wealthy, mysterious, conquering hero. He was returning

1

from the Indies with much gold from Peru. Captain de Soto had not returned since he sailed from Seville twenty-two years earlier. He had been at that time an unknown youth of fourteen who owned only a sword and a buckler. His rise from undistinguished heritage gave hope to me and many a young man in the crowd that day.

I did not meet the Governor until the following year, but I saw him on three occasions at games and tournaments. In one tournament held near his palace estate, I won a mounted sword event, and my prize, a pair of steel gauntlets, was presented to me by the daughter of Pedrarias Davila. The sadistic Pedrarias, by then dead, had been the Governor's early mentor in the Indies. Later, in November, the Governor married the daughter, Isabel, in the city of Valladolid. He thus joined one of the most powerful and richest clans in all of Spain. At age thirty-six Captain de Soto had everything. At least we young men thought that.

With his success and achievements, we believed Hernando de Soto would settle down and enjoy his great wealth and status. We young *hidalgos* discussed his good fortune at length. We'd seen him striding about in his fine clothes and jewelry. None in my circle of friends were invited to his social events, but we thought, what more could any man desire? It was only later that I understood the driving obsession of this man. Each of us forms our own measure for personal success; in the Governor's mind he had not yet achieved his full measure.

During his first year back in Spain, Hernando de Soto was a busy man. After paying his tax to the crown, he purchased his palace and furnished and staffed it befitting a high noble. Amid all this there were the martial tournaments, parties, and gambling. Then he was off to Valladolid for his high-society wedding to Isabel.

However, the Governor's chief mission was arranging a meeting with our sovereign, Charles V. Unfortunately, Charles was off leading his fleet in the capture of Tunis and visiting the Pope. De Soto sought from Charles the documents required to conquer still unexplored territory in the New World. De Soto had great success, but he had been always the number two man behind men like Pedrarias in Panama and Pizarro in Peru. There were still patents to be granted by the crown for the conquest of lands like Colombia and Guatemala. The Governor yearned for his own command and to lead men in the discovery and capture of great fortunes; it had been done by Pizarro with the Incas and Cortes with the Aztecs. There were certainly other golden empires to find, capture, and plunder in the vast New World, and Hernando de Soto applied every ounce of his wealth and charm to become that *adelantado*.

Charles returned to Spain in early 1537, and in April the Governor was granted an audience with the man who was both the Spanish king and the Holy Roman Emperor. Charles, a warrior monarch, enjoyed meeting with his notable conquistador from the Indies. However, the Governor did not get the *capitulacion* he envisioned. Instead, the king granted him permission to invade a land known as *La Florida*.

I never heard the Governor express disappointment with the grant he received, for there were many enticing stories about the fantastic empires in this mysterious land. Besides the *capitulacion*, Charles named Hernando de Soto the Governor of Cuba, and made him a member of the prestigious Knights of Santiago.

For generations my family remained among the privileged class. We were proud that no one with our blood need perform common labors. Some made their mark through military service, going to battle whenever and wherever needed by our sovereign, as my father had. Others became scribes, accountants, and secretaries. I am proud to have mastered two professions: swordsman and scribe.

It was through my work with the quill that I met Father Vicente Castilla. The Father had been with the Governor during his years in Panama and Peru, and he hired me as a scribe when he returned to Seville with the Governor. Through work with the Father I learned much of the habits of the native people in the Indies. Many became slaves; slaves were the chief source of wealth in conquered areas lacking gold or silver. The Father sought better ways to convert these savages. If they became Christians they would likely not be enslaved; otherwise they were regarded as little more than commercial beasts of burden.

Father Castilla was a small, aging Dominican who shaved his entire body. He admired and prayed daily for the Governor. I have heard many of his prayers appealing for help in controlling the Governor's temper and his treatment of Indians. Most of my mornings started with prayer beside the Father. His life was dedicated to saving the souls of the infidels. I'm told his books on conversion are still used by missionaries.

The Governor's private secretary from the Indies was ill and would not accompany him to *La Florida*. Father Castilla arranged an audience for me with the Governor to apply for the position. I met him after a jousting meet in August of 1537. I had previously met with several of his officials, including Captain Luis de Moscoso, his *maestro de campo*. Both Father Castilla and Moscoso, who became a friend and lived here in Mexico until his death two years ago, told me the Governor was intrigued with a secretary who also was a mounted swordsman.

Father Castilla and I waited near the stands, and following the meet we watched as the crowd dispersed. When the Governor saw us approaching, he stood in his great black cape and flashing sword. He came to the rail of the stand; with him were fifteen or twenty of his guards, friends, and aides. I followed the Father. I was leading my horse, Explorer, for Moscoso had said I would be asked to ride.

As we approached the Governor, who wore a red, flat, felt hat trimmed in gold and a gold-embroidered black velvet shirt, I could feel his eyes before I could truly see them. They were cold, black eyes that one never forgot, yet my words fail in their description. He held his head high and seemed to be always looking down. His eyes seldom moved. Rather, his entire head swiveled like that of a hawk eying its prey. His bronze face was strangely handsome, with sharp chiseled features. His coarse, coal-black hair, beard, and mustache were close trimmed and glistened in the late sun. There was a regal air about him that cannot be schooled, but comes only with birth and supreme confidence.

I was an inch taller than the Governor, but he, while taller than most men, was thick and heavy in body and limb, a powerful man. I was said to be handsome in those days, but I was of another build and complexion. I was lean with fair hair and skin, brown eyes, and except for a thin mustache, was clean shaven. I could ride well and handle my sword with the best, perhaps even the Governor himself. However, he was superb on a horse and the best lancer I have ever known.

The Father introduced me, and I stepped forward and removed my black leather riding cap and bowed.

"Father Castilla and Captain Moscoso tell me you can ride and use a sword as well as a pen. Is this so?" His commanding voice came deep and measured, but not loud, his words clear and sharp as his features.

"Yes, sir. It is so."

"Good." His head moved slightly inspecting me. "Mount and behead that joust-mark to the right."

Behind a log fence and over a sand racing track in the jousting field, one white, man-sized figure was still standing untouched.

I was confident. I mounted Explorer. Explorer easily cleared the fence and I raced him seventy yards to the left and turned. I brought him to his hind legs and then raced him toward the target. Drawing my sword, I beheaded it with ease, then turned and again galloped back toward it. At full gallop I threw my sword from thirty feet. The sword imbedded in the dummy's chest. This was a maneuver that few knights could do with a heavy weapon over three feet in length. I'd practiced it for years.

I returned to the reviewing stands and had Explorer bow to the Governor. There was clapping by some of his entourage, but it stopped when the Governor turned his head ever so slightly.

"Ranjel, is it?"

"Yes, sir."

"Well, Ranjel, that was quite an act." For the first time, I saw him smile. His lips turned up only very slightly, showing large white teeth, but his teeth remained together. I never saw him with an open-mouthed smile.

I tipped my hat.

"On Wednesday report to my office on the pier. Captain Moscoso will make your arrangements."

Without further talk, Hernando de Soto, the Governor of Cuba and *Adelantado* of *La Florida*, stood and headed for his carriages.

Within a few weeks, I would be with this man until his death more than any other human being. Despite the tragic results, and some tormenting dreams, I remain proud of those years of service. It altered my life forever.

•

Rodrigo Ranjel, often spelled Rangel, was thirty years old when he first met de Soto in 1537. While he was educated and talented he was not wealthy, for de Soto paid his entrada *expenses. This was not true for most of de Soto's officers and officials. They paid their own way and brought their own staffs. We know that de Soto was fond of Ranjel, for the secretary was mentioned in his will, and likely due to this inheritance was later able to live well in Mexico. There was an added bond between the two men since both were Castilians from a common area in southern Extremadura near Portugal.*

When Ranjel uses the word entrada *he is referring to the expedition itself. A* capitulacion *is the royal grant de Soto needed from Charles to permit the conquest, and* adelantado *is the honorary name, a carryover from the Middle Ages, given the commander going into the new frontier. While Charles would give no money toward the* entrada, *one of the conditions of the* capitulacion *was that one fifth of all plunder be given to the crown. For this reason officials from Charles' treasury would accompany the expedition.*

We have some evidence that Ranjel did some other writing later in his life. Two papers have been found relating to his interest in the life of Alexander the Great.

La Florida to the Spanish was what is now most of southeastern United States. It was discovered and named on Easter Sunday of 1513 by Juan Ponce de León.

Chapter 2

I write from the courtyard of my home in the City of Mexico, winnowing my notes and memories into a history of the *entrada*. I need not repeat what others have written and is common knowledge throughout Spain about the Governor and *La Florida*.

The eight months from the time I signed my agreement as personal secretary until we sailed for Cuba in April of 1538 were hectic. I worked with many people at the pier and at the army mustering post near the coast in Andalusia. I worked with the Governor; his wife, Isabel; Alonso de Ayala, the Governor's majordomo; and Juan de Anasco, a mariner and astrologer, to plan the voyage. Captain Moscoso and a young captain from the Governor's Peru days, Juan Ruiz Lobillo, were out recruiting *hidalgos*. In the end there were more men and officers wanting passage to *La Florida* than there were berths. One reason for this was the arrival in Spain during the fall of 1537 of Cabeza de Vaca.

De Vaca was the royal treasurer with a four-hundred-man force that sailed from Cuba to *La Florida* nearly ten years earlier in 1528. These four hundred men and eighty horses had disappeared without a trace. The ill-equipped and ill-managed force was led by the one-eyed veteran of Cuban conquest, Pánfilo de Narváez. De Vaca was one of only three survivors who nine years later found their way into Spanish Mexico.

The cantankerous little man reported to Charles V, and

later visited several times with the Governor. He provided useful information on the topography and native peoples of the land. According to de Vaca, it was not a welcoming land. It went from swampy and hot to dry and cold, and many of the natives were unfriendly and fierce warriors. However, he left plenty of hints of great hidden wealth in the interior of this forbidding land. In fact, when his relatives asked his advice, he told them to sell everything they owned and join the *entrada*. Without some special knowledge, why would a man give that advice?

I believe that the tattooed, wrinkled man was bitter that the Governor had been granted the *capitulacion* that he thought was due him. He was offered a position with the armada, but he declined. Meanwhile, the entire country was awash with gossip about the great wealth to be had in *La Florida*. Hernando de Soto was a proven leader who had returned to Spain with a ton of gold; in addition, he owned land, silver mines, and slaves in the Indies. Now he was going into a new territory, likely with even more riches. Every man's thoughts followed the same path to easy plunder and a huge personal *repartimiento*. Gold fever and greed swept our land, and I confess to its firm grip on me. Greed is the father of many false dreams.

I was in several meetings with the Governor and de Vaca, and the Governor, after hearing the man's tale of starvation, ordered tons of hardtack, cured meats, olive oil, and wine. The Governor's plan was to gather many of his final supplies in Cuba, but he understood that many European-made items he needed were not available there. One necessity he would pick up in Cuba was horses. I was disappointed, for I had to leave Explorer.

While he never said so, I'm sure de Soto was glad de Vaca did not accept his offer to join the force. De Soto wanted to gather around him men who would not question his command, and it was clear de Vaca was not such a man.

De Soto spent much of his time during this period selecting his senior officers, and I believe he did a fine job. These men would lead the over-six-hundred-man army. The second-in-command of the army at the start would be a Peru colleague, Nuño de Tobar. Moscoso would be in charge of organizing and guarding the camps, the *maestro de campo*. Soto's personal guards of some sixty halberdiers were commanded by Cristóbal de Espindola.

I always addressed Hernando de Soto as Governor, but his officers, at his request, addressed him as Soto. Therefore, as I proceed I will generally refer to him as Soto. These officers and others contributed to the armada and paid for their arms, uniforms, foods, wines, etc. Many also paid for servants, slaves, wives, and concubines. Most women would remain on the ships.

Much of my work was helping Anasco and Isabel with the purchase of European-made items such as iron chain links and collars for newly captured slaves and porters and dozens of other steel and iron items such as strap containers, picks, and spades. Other items included gunpowder, chain mail, harquebuses, crossbows, Indian trade goods, and the lists went on and on.

Soto was experienced and knew the hardships he would face; he would be prepared for everything—everything, I now understand, but the failure to find the treasures he sought. Our lives would have been very different if we had found another Inca city.

During this period Soto purchased six large ships and three brigantines and manned them with pilots and crews. The *capitulacion* that Soto signed with Charles was a lengthy document drawn up by lawyers from both sides. It required Soto to take at least five hundred men, including priests for the instruction of the natives. There were three main issues: the taxes to be paid, the size of the territory covered by the grant, and the time Soto would have to complete the mission. The land to be explored would be the same as granted Narváez. Soto would be given four years to accomplish his mission, which included building forts and establishing colonies, and of course reporting back to Charles. For all of us it was a grand and exciting time.

Finally, on April 1, 1538, Soto had his officers muster the army of volunteers near a quay at the mouth of the Guadalquivir River. I accompanied him and six of his top officers as we rode down to where nearly one thousand recruits had been mustered. They were in groups of fifty to sixty men with junior officers in charge. I thought the ranks looked splendid in the colorful mixed finery of their silks and sashes.

Following Soto, we rode down the length of the mustered men and turned back. Something in the way Soto turned told me the muster was not going well. Soto, without looking right or left, broke his mount into a canter, and we followed him back to his headquarters tent. He dismounted and strode into the tent, taking a seat at the head of a heavy table. Not a word was spoken, but his face was a metallic mask of fury that I would see often during the next four years. He held out his hands palms up for us to take seats at both sides of the table. His arms and hands were thick and powerful, his wrists circled with broad gold bands. The faces of his officers were like gravestones. Upon seeing his dark eyes and set jaw, a ripple of trepidation spread through me. When we were all seated, he brought his hands down, pounding the table with all his force. For a moment his head and eyes shifted from one side of the table to the other.

"What is this? Are we preparing to visit the old men of the *Casa de Contratación* or perhaps the choir maidens gathered at the Giralda Tower?" His voice was low and cutting, like wind bending winter cane.

Two pages entered the tent carrying pitchers of water and goblets. His head and eyes turned to them for an instant, and then his massive forearm swept the pewter utensils from both of their trays. Quickly gathering up the mess, the startled pages cowered out of the tent. Soto's officers studied the grain and sheen of the command table.

"Tomorrow let us find if we have men ready to fight." He hammered his fist on the table. "I remind you we go to conquer and fight, and Castilians fight in armor. We will take only men equipped and prepared for battle."

He sat back in his chair and took a deep breath, his arms folded across his chest.

"Now go, and correct this mess. We prepare for war, not for a wedding." His voice then became one of a patient father, and he smiled. I still have a dream where I see that smile, teeth together, lips apart but pulled straight back. It said to all: "Go, but be very careful, my friends."

We left without a word.

The following day I spent with Soto and his senior officers going through the ranks and weeding out the weak and ill-equipped. The men selected were told to report to one of the six ships for the official oath and log-in. I watched Soto and his officers break rusty pikes and stomp flat rusty old helmets, shields, and even a few breastplates. Soto challenged several small or frail men by tearing their pikes from their hands or pushing them to the ground, then eliminating them. He also passed a few big, powerful men who pleaded that they lacked money for better equipment; he agreed to equip some. We worked into the night. It was a long day, but Soto was pleased.

ᾧ

On Sunday, April 7th, after Mass and a fine meal, trumpets sounded and several rounds of artillery were fired, and the armada sailed into the Ocean Sea. We were accompanied by twenty ships heading for Vera Cruz in Mexico on a separate mission. It was my first time on the ocean, and I fortunately experienced no sickness. However, the first night out our flagship became entangled with one of the Mexico-bound ships, but it is too long a story to tell and there were no life nor vessels lost. Soto was furious, giving the order to behead the responsible captain. Cooler heads talked him into a change of mind.

In fifteen days we reached the Canaries and stopped for food and water.

Thinking of those early days at sea, I remember a young *hidalgo* that I befriended on my ship, the *San Cristobal*. Gil Evio Tapia had a boyish face of sixteen years, and was the owner of a fine silver-haired greyhound. Two days before reaching the Canaries the dog, at play, was lost overboard. Tapia was heartbroken, for we could not turn back.

Several days later in the Canaries, Tapia spotted his greyhound. It seems that after swimming several hours he had been picked up by a small fishing vessel, but the new owner, believing the dog was a symbol of luck, would not give him up. Again, Tapia despaired. Three days after we sailed from the Canaries, a swinging boom struck the luckless Tapia in the head and swept him overboard. The unconscious youth was wearing armor and sank like an anvil.

I can still see his boyish face.

•

The hidalgos *(basically gentry or noblemen) de Soto recruited were men, poor and rich, but noble, who had been trained for war. Some had fought in the* Reconquista *(Reconquest) in Africa, but that centuries-old crusade against the infidels had ended in Europe in the late fifteenth century. Others had fought in the New World and wanted to return to gain additional honor and wealth. For the younger men the New World was the place to go to gain the personal valor and riches they sought. Second sons, like de Soto and Ranjel, received no inheritance.*

These were tough men of action, unafraid of hardship and danger. They thought of themselves more as Christians than Spaniards. They were quick to defend their personal honor, and were fascinated by ceremony and magical happenings. They were more medieval and identified more with their home regions than Spain, for Spain was not a nation state as it is today. The men and officers considered themselves on a divine mission, but their true goals were conquest, gold, and personal valor. Each man would be given a specific share or repartimiento *of the expedition profits.*

Chapter 3

On the seventh of June, 1538, we anchored in the harbor of Santiago on the eastern end of Cuba. We would be on the island almost one year before we would sail for *La Florida*. I traveled the length of Cuba with its new governor on his administrative duties. We endured heat, mountains, swamps, mosquitoes, storms, and strange foods before reaching Havana. There we would complete our purchase of horses, foods, and other supplies.

Soto had to deal with a matter of concern to all of us with dreams of sharing the plunder of *La Florida*. It involved the Spanish viceroy of Mexico, Don Antonia de Mendoza. He was sending a party led by Vázquez de Coronado into eastern Mexico. Coronado's force could easily end up in *La Florida*. A meeting of two Spanish conquistadors could result in an ugly clash. This had happened in Nicaragua and Peru, and Soto had been involved in that fighting. He and Mendoza both understood the danger and agreed to avoid a clash by having Coronado and his men explore only to the north of Mexico.

Meanwhile, Soto sent Anasco with three brigantines to scout the coast of *La Florida* for a favorable landing spot and to capture Indians for use as guides and interpreters.

It was again a busy time, and as the days drew near to departure I aided the Governor in writing his lengthy will. I am pleased to write that I was one of only a handful of non-family members provided

17

for; he also included his three illegitimate children from the New World. I also worked with other documents, one making Isabel the acting governor of Cuba in Soto's absence.

Several officers and men joined Soto's force in Cuba, while a few Castilians decided to stay on the island. While the officers of the military force were mostly Spanish *hidalgos*, there were also dozens of mercenaries and other peasant soldiers, as well as numerous artisans in the force that included blacksmiths, cooks, shoemakers, tailors, swineherds, and others, including slaves and porters.

ॐ

We sailed from Havana on May 18, 1539, and every man and woman on the nine vessels sailing north had faith in the man who was our leader, Hernando de Soto. I mention women for there were a few wives, servants, whores, and concubines, plus some female artisans, but most women would remain with the ships.

I stood on the main deck as the *San Cristóbal* cleared the harbor of Havana, and I can still picture the figure of the Governor standing by his helmsman and pilot. He wore a polished steel helmet with a white plume and a black and gold cape, silhouetted against a brilliant Indies sky. He and every one of us were confident that we would find a golden empire greater than any yet discovered. Soto was a man much admired and much feared. On that day we all would have followed this dark and driven man into hell's own flames. Little did I know that day that of the more than six hundred men to go ashore in *La Florida* only half would survive.

ॐ

My first view of *La Florida* was a quivering green line on the horizon. It was May 25. During the next days the Governor's frustration grew as we labored along sandy islands and a shallow, tree-choked coast, trying to find the broad natural harbor Anasco had scouted earlier (though he had failed to capture any Indians to use as guides). From time to time we saw plumes of smoke which we knew to be Indian signals. At last, days later, after heated meetings between Soto and Anasco, failed scouting parties, and grounded vessels, we reached a broad but shallow harbor where Soto finally decided to establish a base camp. It took several days to unload and transport the men, over two hundred horses, swine, and a mountain of equipment and supplies ashore.

We established our camp at an Indian village near the shore of the bay. The village, named Ozita after its *cacique* (chief), was on a small river and consisted of seven sizable wood and thatched houses that had been abandoned upon our arrival. The Indians were in great fear of us, for they had experienced cruel treatment years earlier by the party of Pánfilo de Narváez. Both the *cacique*'s house and a burial temple at the opposite end of the village were built on large manmade mounds. Soto immediately ordered the surrounding forest to be cleared to the distance of a crossbow shot. This was done to prevent sneak attacks and give better advantage to our horses. The logs from the forest were used to build a palisade of earth and timber along the stream for the storage of our supplies.

On June 3, Soto, who occupied the *cacique*'s house, dressed in his finest armor and marched to the beach to take formal possession of this land for our Emperor Charles V and for himself. He raised the purple and gold banner of His Caesarean Majesty and named the bay "Bay of Holy Spirit." We then kneeled and prayed with Father Castilla, who was holding a golden cross and accompanied by his twelve velvet-robed priests.

‌჻

As the hot, humid days passed, Soto's impatience grew with the inability to capture and retain knowledgeable Indians for use as guides and interpreters. We all were eager to get on the road to the golden city of a second Inca empire, for we were disappointed in the primitive village of Ozita. In the village all that had been found were a few freshwater pearls. These low-grade pearls were found among the bones of the infidels in the temple-ossuary.

Scouting parties, mounted and afoot, were sent out in all directions looking for additional villages, Indians, and food. The local Ozita villagers remained hidden in the swamps and thick forests, where they used their long bows with great skill. These were bows as thick as an arm and as tall as a man, and they were deadly at up to two hundred paces. A few natives were captured, but one of our foot soldiers was killed when an unseen assailant sent an arrow through his steel gorget and into his throat. Two horses also died of wounds, but the horses were of little use in the swamps and thick vine-tangled forests surrounding the village.

‌჻

Captain Luis de Moscoso and I sat at the evening fire trying to ward off the swarming mosquitoes. We were together often in our close work with the Governor. That night, as was frequently the case, we were joined by Don Carlos Enriquez, a young cavalryman who was married to Soto's niece. All of us were from an area of Extremadura near the city of Badajoz.

"Pedro," Don Carlos said, taking a seat by the smoky fire, "has returned from patrol saying the native guide misled him." Pedro Calderón was one of the young *hidalgos*.

"Ah," Moscoso said, removing a blanket from over his head. "Has he told Soto?" Moscoso was my age, but built like Soto.

"That is what I heard." Don Carlos was ten years our junior, but had a mature, calming manner.

"Anyone want to wager a ducat?" Moscoso asked, whistling softly.

"On what?" I asked.

"The guide will die tonight, but the wager is on how he dies."

"How do you know he dies?" Don Carlos asked. He had brought his new wife to Cuba, but she remained there.

"I was with Soto in Peru," Moscoso said, turning his gray eyes from Don Carlos back to the fire, "and I know what is needed and how our leader thinks. The natives must understand what happens when they betray us." There was a slight smile on his handsome face.

"Perhaps he'll be whipped," Don Carlos said.

Moscoso chuckled. "This is not a schoolyard, nor Soto a schoolmaster."

"What then, Luis?" I asked.

"The war dogs need meat," Moscoso said, staring into the smoke.

"Is it true about those dogs of that madman Calcanas?" Don Carlos asked.

"They're not for herding swine; they would eat them. Calcanas has trained them to kill for their food."

Don Carlos and I studied Luis. He was right.

~

Within an hour, Soto gathered the remaining guides together. They needed to understand what happened when they deceived their masters. Soto had learned from Pedrarias, his brutal mentor in Panama, that quick action and fear are keys in establishing control of the natives.

He had the errant guide stripped naked, and for his defense he was given a walking stick. His fellow guides watched as he was led into a large, torch-lit area surrounded by armed soldiers. There he would defend himself against three war dogs. These huge, hungry mastiffs wore spiked collars and had been bred for killing. Seeing the restrained dogs, the young infidel crouched ready with his stick. The dog-handlers and the dogs knew the procedure.

The first dog released dashed for the guide and quickly fastened the stick in its powerful jaws. As the man and dog pulled and wrestled for the stick, the other two beasts were released. They raced for the victim and went directly for his genitals and underbelly with their powerful jaws. In an instant the screaming native was disemboweled. He fell howling, entangled in his own gut as he rolled over several times. He attempted to crawl off, but the ravenous killers were eating him alive.

In the morning the other guides were made to gather the skull and the gnawed and scattered bones of their friend. It was a lesson none would forget.

The manifest listed over twenty-one dogs shipped from Havana. This did not include pet animals, but were the war dogs and those used by the swineherds. Soto brought a herd of some forty swine which traveled with us. The war dogs, mostly Irish wolfhounds and greyhounds, were a part of our force during the entire *entrada,* and next to the horses proved a significant factor in our mastery of the native warriors and their leaders.

The execution of the guide by the dogs was the first of several I witnessed during the *entrada.* It was disturbing to me then, and remains so.

I prayed with Father Castilla the following morning, and he assured me that the guides had been read the *Requerimento,* and that this was a just war to enlighten and convert them from their idol worship. He regretted that he had not completed his work with this man, but the guides now understood to give fealty to their masters or face destruction.

There were no more troubles with these guides, but it would remain a problem at many tribal villages throughout the expedition.

●

At the age of eighteen after four years in Panama, de Soto formed a compañero *with two other conquistadors. This was a form of personal and business partnership where each of the partners share virtually everything in common, now and in the future. De Soto remained until his death in the partnership with one of the partners. This brotherhood made a good deal of sense in places like Panama in those times. A man needs allies in a violent, winner-take-all world. De Soto's paranoid predecessor Pedrarias was famous for executing his own men. He had beheaded his own son-in-law, Balboa, and left his head mounted on a pole.*

De Soto and his two partners were very wealthy men, but not all of their wealth came from the plunder of Inca gold. Much of their wealth came during their years in Nicaragua from the brutal enslavement and sale of the local natives. Hernando de Soto was not just a fearless adventurer. We see from Ranjel's story of the dogs that de Soto was a man of action—strong, brutal, and driven.

The Requerimento was an edict from the earlier days of King Ferdinand that allowed only the enslavement of hostile Indians. It was often read to the uncomprehending natives by the priests, but it was generally ignored by the conquistadors, including de Soto. Enslaving the native people was a major part of Spanish plunder.

It is believed that de Soto first made landfall in the southern part of what is now Tampa Bay.

Chapter 4

I had nearly a year in Cuba to adjust to the heat, humidity, mosquitoes, and poor indigenous foods, but in *La Florida* we needed to wear armor or risk a deadly Ozita arrow. It was an unpleasant adjustment to agonizing heat. Every man had a different combination of armor that he had acquired over the years, some from the dead on the battlefields of Europe or Africa. In camp I wore only my padded jacket, but when on patrol I wore a mail shirt over the jacket, and an open-faced, wide-brim *morrión*. I used heavy leather skirts for my mount. The horse I was assigned was a rugged little chestnut from Barbary Coast stock. I named him Boot, for he had a white left leg that resembled a woman's fancy boot. Boot was with me throughout the *entrada*. I would not be here today except for Boot, but of that I will write later.

Frustration grew with the passage of each sweltering day. Without an interpreter it was difficult to tell what the few captives we obtained were attempting to say, but to me one young man seemed to be saying that he knew of a Spaniard living among the Indians. However, that young Indian escaped his second night in camp, and when it was discovered that he had been helped in his escape by his mother, the Governor had the handsome woman thrown to the dogs. When Soto gave orders like this, I would see the flash of rage in his eyes, but his manner and voice were like he was asking for a second plate of meat.

That afternoon I was invited to Soto's quarters for wine with several of his lead captains. It started as a somber affair, for one of the captains had an eye for the woman Soto fed to the dogs. The mood changed suddenly when a messenger from one of the patrols rode up with word that they had captured a Spanish-speaking Indian.

"Did you see this man?" Soto asked the sweating, breathless messenger.

"Oh yes, sir, he looks just like the rest of those savages. His group was all painted red with a bunch of feathers on their heads. But this one ran forward shouting that he was a Christian from Seville, and giving the sign of the cross. He pleaded not to kill his Indian friends, for he said they had saved him from torture and death. The captain said he would have him and the whole group here by morning. In all there are ten of them, but one is wounded."

We were overjoyed by this news, and with a rare smile Soto ordered more wine and directed me to mark this day as special in my journal. It was June 12, 1539.

Juan Ortiz arrived the next morning, weathered, tattooed, and dressed like his native friends. Over the next several days his tale of twelve years of captivity and survival slowly evolved.

Juan and I were the same age with similar noble heritages. We would become friends until his death. My journal during this period has many passages relating to Juan's story as it unfolded. I have welded these notes together in Juan's own words as he spoke to me, the Governor, and others. He became a regular member of our small campfire group.

᠅

"I was born in Seville of noble parents. My father was the magistrate of the city's Christian burial grounds, and my mother tutored young men in Latin. I had been well educated when in 1526 I sailed for Cuba at the age of sixteen. I became a page for Pánfilo de Narváez and his wife. Two years later Narváez led a party of some three hundred men and forty horses on an *entrada* into *La Florida*. Within a month the entire party had disappeared.

"Several months later I was part of a ship's crew sent by Narváez's wife in the hope of locating some word of the missing *entrada*.

"I recall the beautiful day we arrived at the bay where Narváez had disembarked. The pale green water was like a mirror. Four friendly Indians canoed out and boarded our ship. They said that our friends had left a message for us in a tree. With our glass we could see what looked like a letter imbedded in the fork of a tree off a deep sandy beach. The captain asked that the Indians go and bring us the message, but they refused, saying they were warned never to touch it. They offered to row us to the shore, but our captain refused. The captain, a veteran of many campaigns, believed we could not trust these Indians. However, three of us younger men believed there was little danger and volunteered to go ashore for the message with the friendly Indians. The captain told us he thought we were making a mistake, but he would not stop us. He did demand that two of the Indians stay on the ship. I remember thinking the captain was getting too old and had lost his nerve.

"We beached the canoe on the sandy shore and the five of us walked slowly toward the area where the message was located. The two Indians were talking and laughing, and nothing could be seen in the thick, tangled growth of the forest. Up the beach seagulls were quarrelling over food.

"When we were within ten yards of the tree, the forest exploded and we were quickly surrounded by fifty armed and shouting Indians. I was stunned, shocked. One of my shipmates broke through their circle and started running for the canoe. He hadn't gone twenty yards before he fell with a half-dozen arrows in his neck, back, and buttocks. I glanced at our ship and saw the two Indians left there dive overboard and escape. Meanwhile, two Indians reached our fallen man now trying to crawl to the water, and they beat his head in with war clubs. The savages, wearing only loin cloths, shouted their approval, threatening my friend and me with bows and arrows and jabbing us with clubs and spears. All went quiet when their *cacique*, a big, heavy man named Ozita, stepped forward. He was a man without a nose. Later, I learned that his nose had been cut off by Narváez because he could not lead them to gold. For the same reason, Ozita's number-one wife was thrown to the dogs. Need I tell you that he was a very bitter man, hating all Christians and bearded men?

"The *cacique* then pushed my remaining partner, Raúl, a rugged *hidalgo* from Valladolid, into the ring and shouted orders to his men. The warriors began shooting arrows at Raúl's feet, forcing him to dance, jump, and run about in their circle. At first it seemed like an amusing game, but then with a word from Ozita, one by one the arrows began to pierce the dancing Raúl. The savages were chanting and at a shout from the *cacique* another arrow would be shot into Raúl. The game, I soon understood, was to slowly fill the hopping Raúl with arrows but keep him alive and moving as long as possible. The savages would cheer with a clever shot through an ear or Raúl's nose. During this period, I looked out to sea and saw our ship leaving the harbor at full sail. My heart sank; I prayed for a quick death.

"Finally, Raúl stood swaying back and forth with a least a dozen arrows in him, his shirt and pants dripping blood. He could dance no more. Ozita stepped forward and the chanting stopped. Two older warriors came around to face Raúl, readying their arrows. My shipmate had stopped screaming, but his eyes were open. At a word from the *cacique* both savages released their arrows. One arrow entered his throat, the other his chest. He fell over backwards, hitting the sand with a thud. Blessedly, Raúl was dead; the savages cheered.

"But Raúl was not dead. The savages went silent as he struggled to his feet, and he started staggering toward the *cacique*. It was surreal. Several of the infidels cried out in fear and disbelief. I could see the arrow completely through his neck. The *cacique* rushed forward, bashing him in the head with his club. Raúl fell forward onto the blood-covered sand like a sack of meal.

"The *cacique* came and grabbed me by the arm and forced me out into the ring. The savages cheered and stomped their feet. They shook their bows; blood was in their eyes. I prayed aloud to St. Mary for a swift death. I cannot find words for that feeling of hopeless dread that filled me at that moment. We walked out to where Raúl's body still lay, his eyes staring into a cloudless sky. I walked and stood with the *cacique* as if in a trance. My body seemed foreign, numb, detached from my mind.

"It was then that I heard the shouting of different voices, and the cheering dwindled away. Four women had pushed through into the ring, shouting at the *cacique*. I later learned that it was the *cacique*'s number-two wife and his three daughters. They pleaded for my life, saying I was more valuable as a slave, and that I was not responsible for the loss of his wife or his nose. I was, of course, much relieved, but many times during the next year I wished that I had died that day with Raúl.

"Ozita proved a bitter and very erratic man. For weeks I would do my hard but routine slave duties, and then Ozita would be reminded of his nose or his wife and call for me to be punished. Several times he had me run through the village from sunup to sundown, and if I stopped his men were told to shoot me. Another time he had me roasted like a pig over hot embers. Again his wife and daughters pleaded for me. That time it took me weeks to recover from bleeding blisters the size of oranges.

"At one time I was told to guard the tribe's burial ground. It was their practice to place the dead in crude wooden coffins that were left on top of the ground, and often at night the deceased would be carried off by wild animals. I was told if any bodies were taken I would be burned to death.

"One night I fell asleep and the body of a child dead two days was carried off by a panther. I woke when I heard the wooden lid hit the ground. I was too late; the child's body was gone. I had been given two small spears as weapons to use, and I was able to follow the beast by the moonlight. After a time I came to a spot where I could hear gnawing and chewing from behind some bushes. The best I could think was to launch my spears in that direction. I did, and I was encouraged by a "salty" feel to my throwing hand. When first light came I found that I had miraculously killed the panther. For a few weeks I was not mistreated, for the tribe honored anyone who kills a panther by his own hand.

"Killing the panther did not satisfy Ozita for long. One day his daughter came to me and said because of bad relations with a neighboring *cacique*, her father was going to sacrifice me to the sun gods by burning me alive. That night she helped me escape to a neighboring tribe where the *cacique* was named Mocozo. I lived with Mocozo as one of the tribe members for over ten years, until I met the Spanish soldiers."

•

Because of the heat and humidity most conquistadors did not wear the full body armor popular in sixteenth-century Europe. It was just too hot. Many wore mail shirts or just an escaupil, *which was a padded jacket of cotton-stuffed canvas. These were quite effective against the native's cane arrows. Poison arrows were not used in La Florida as they were in Central America. Ranjel's* morrión *was a steel open-faced helmet with a sharp crest and wide brim.*

Horses were very useful in controlling the natives in the New World. They had not been seen there and were frightening and effective in open-area conflicts. Most of de Soto's horses were a North African breed, with strong legs and hard bones.

Indian cultures varied considerably throughout La Florida. Most, however, had one dominant cacique *with loose control over several other* caciques *paying tribute to him. There was a continual struggle for control within these groups, and also between the larger dominant groups. The world of most Indians was not wide-ranging, perhaps twenty-five miles. They normally could not venture safely into neighboring* caciques' *territories.*

Chapter 5

The Governor outfitted Juan Ortiz with clothes and a horse, but it was weeks before Juan could adjust to clothes. He had lived too long as an Indian.

Juan was questioned by Soto and others. We were disappointed to learn he did not know of cities of gold. Still, Soto reminded us, he had never traveled more than thirty miles from Mocozo's villages. He did explain that both of the warring *caciques,* Ozita and Mocozo, paid tribute to a more powerful *cacique,* Urriparacoxi. This prosperous *cacique* ruled ninety miles to the northeast in a maize-growing area.

The Governor found optimism in Juan's report. He sent Baltasar de Gallegos, one of his respected captains, with Juan, to find Urriparacoxi. He lectured the men that where there was maize, it had been his experience from Peru, it would eventually lead to cities with gold.

Meanwhile, Soto sent the bigger ships back to Havana and prepared the main force for marching. He would leave a small force and the smaller ships at the harbor to guard the supplies. He now had general directions and would be off to find a winter campsite with an ample food supply, for there was little food in the low, sandy areas near the coast, and feeding over seven hundred people was a major concern.

De Gallegos' messengers reported back that they had found

maize and had captured a few natives, but Urriparacoxi and his people were hiding in the swamps. The captain actually sent two reports, one for Soto's eyes only. The letter shared with the men rumored that gold and other riches were to be found to the west in a city called Ocale. With our spirits lifted, the march began. Soto's plan was to winter in Ocale.

I rode with Soto and his small group of advance horsemen. It was slow, hellish travel through a tangled swamp forest, and always there was the threat of ambush. There was little food, and after inching slowly ahead for nearly a week, Soto suspected malice. He quickly had four of our five guides thrown to the dogs. The trail improved, but the heat, mud, and mosquitoes remained.

Soto, eager to reach the golden city of Ocale, had us riding well ahead of the main army. He was a leader with no fear for his personal safety. On two occasions I rode back to the main force to get additional horsemen. It was a dangerous mission, for Indians were everywhere, but I was proud to serve the Governor. I was one of his best and trusted horsemen.

჻

"Our God rides with you, my friend," Luis de Moscoso said. Soto had placed Moscoso in charge of the main army in his absence. Despite the heat he wore three-quarter blackened armor with an open-faced helmet. The sweat ran down his head as he examined three cane arrows that he had pulled out of the back of my padded doublet. He handed them to me; one had a fishbone tip, and the other two were sharpened cane. I assumed that both cane tips had been split by my mail shirt.

"It was the doublet, not the mail, that saved you."

"Have you some meal for Boot?" I asked. "We start back in an hour; he will not make it without a good mix." Moscoso gave me his devilish smile.

"Ah, I like a man who thinks of his mount's belly before his own. I have some meal hidden; I'm afraid if the men find it they'll eat it." I followed him to a pack animal, and he dumped a good ration of mix in my sack.

"How is the Governor?" he asked.

"Impatient . . . like a man dancing on a stove lid."

"Of course. He smells the gold."

"God, gold, and glory," I said, leaning on Boot as he ate.

"You scribblers ponder too much. I'll dig out a weevil-filled biscuit and some cheese for you."

"Have you been eating from the ship's store?"

"Hell, you know better. I eat with the men: roots, acorns, and cabbage palmettos. Tell Soto that the men are growling like bears . . . not about lack of gold, it's about food . . . but he knows I can handle them." He smiled. "Still, we need food. If you find maize, tell him to send some back, for the men and animals are growing weak. How is the trail ahead?"

"He threw four guides to the dogs," I said. Moscoso knew my thoughts.

"Talk to Father, if it helps. The Governor must do what is needed to bring God's will to the idol worshippers. They must serve us without question. The devil is in them and the dogs are needed. Besides, the dogs must eat too." He had that smile again. "But what of the trail?"

"I've been to my knees in mud, and to my chin in water. I swam alongside Boot twice, but at those streams we cut trees for the footmen." Moscoso removed his helmet and mopped his face and head with a huge red rag.

"Sometimes," he said, "I think of Seville and a cool pitcher and a warm woman." We chuckled. In many ways he was like Soto, but he yearned more for the easy life that Soto had forsaken. There were few men with the single focus of the Governor; he was driven and it was not our God or the gold that focused him—it was his will dedicated to a quest for power.

ॐ

Armed with sufficient cavalry to conquer Ocale, Soto pushed north. I had rejoined him and at times I slept in the saddle. At my age as I write, I would not last a day.

Ocale proved no city of gold; rather, it was a larger abandoned village of palm-thatched houses. It did, however, have a supply of maize, plus a few beans, pumpkins, and squash. We sent maize back for Moscoso and the footmen, and we waited and rested. The men were worn and disappointed, and they pondered that after eight weeks we had uncovered no hints of gold or other wealth.

Soto tried persuasion in an attempt to draw the Ocale *cacique* from hiding in the snarled forest, but it did not work, nor did threatening reprisals. This tough *cacique,* however, did not remain silent, nor did he tell us we could find gold by moving on to another territory. Instead, he was defiant, and he replied by messengers that he knew the evil intent of the Spanish invaders and would fight to the last man to defend his country. He managed to capture three of our men and he had them beheaded. Their sectioned bodies were hung in the trees for the birds.

While there was food at Ocale, it was not adequate for the winter months, nor had we been able to capture enough natives to do our camp work. Thus, Soto decided to move northwest, leading a smaller force of fifty horsemen and one hundred footmen. Moscoso would remain at Ocale with the main army.

We now entered a country spaced with a mix of dry savanna and forests of towering longleaf pine and gum. Traveling with the mounted vanguard, we were able to find some game, fruits, and acorns among undergrowth of dogwood and holly. We traveled quickly from one abandoned village to the next.

From the few natives we captured we learned that this is where Narváez's doomed party had become lost. Moving in the direction we were moving and near starvation, they were attacked ahead and decimated by the ferocious Apalachee.

⁂

The predawn air was wet and heavy as I adjusted the saddle onto Boot. We had camped in an abandoned village and the vanguard was preparing to move on to the northwest.

"Ranjel, we would like an audience with his Excellency." I turned to face three cavalrymen and three footmen. The spokesman was a footman named Bartolo; he was an older respected veteran of African campaigns.

The Governor had not emerged from the hut where he had slept.

"Very well, I have not seen him. Let me see." The request did not surprise me, for I had heard the men talking for several days.

"Wait here." I walked over to Soto's hut; it was built on a mound and was the largest in the village.

"Governor, are you awake?"

"Yes."

"Bartolo, the footman, and five other men would like to talk to you."

It seemed like a long time before he answered. "Have them wait."

I finished saddling Boot and waited with the men. After some time the Governor came out of his hut followed by two pages. He was ready to ride wearing a polished burgonet and a red-studded brigandine. His sword was at his side. He marched straight toward us.

"Good morning, men. A fine day to march. What can I do for you?" He gave us his teeth-clenched smile. Bartolo stepped forward, saluting.

"Excellency, the men have asked that I speak for the group."

Soto nodded his head. "Proceed." The Governor's head and eyes were moving from man to man.

"We know from the reports of Cabeza de Vaca that the difficult Apalachee country is ahead and that there was no gold found in their territory. We also know that many in Narváez's army died there and very few made an escape. We therefore would like to consider returning to our supply ships and seeking a favorable place to establish a Spanish Christian settlement. We have traveled over three hundred miles and found no hint of gold or silver. We believe there is no gold in *La Florida*, only tribe after tribe of hostile Indians."

Soto stepped forward with his head held high, looking down as his dark eyes surveyed the group. Several of the men studied the tops of their boots.

"I promised none of you an easy or hastily earned bag of gold," Soto said. "Your *repartimiento* will come, but it is more one of individual will and courageous endurance. I remind you that I was twenty-two years in the Indies before returning to Spain a wealthy man. Also, I advise not to accept the old rumors and reports of others. See with your own eyes. We are well prepared for this mission. Our army cannot be beaten. Each of us must give the needed time and effort. We will succeed. Now go and prepare to march. The day is young. The time is now. We will find gold."

•

Experts believe that the production of maize was important to the development of Indian societies. Those tribes who grew maize and other crops had more time to organize other productive activities than the hunter-gatherers. This included improvements in warfare, artifacts, accumulating wealth, and gaining control of others.

De Soto was certainly not pleased that the Indian villages were abandoned and the caciques were in hiding. In Peru and Central America he had learned that to control a tribe you must capture and control their cacique.

While De Soto was, perhaps uncharacteristically, patient in listening to the concerns of his men, entrada decisions were not made by consensus. Hernando de Soto was in control and his will prevailed.

Chapter 6

I leaned back on my saddle, which rested against the outside of a huge circular hut. I was finishing my day's journal in another abandoned Indian village; we had passed through several villages during the week since leaving Ocale, all abandoned. Flooding afternoon rains had forced Soto to halt the march; he was napping in the hut as he often did during these tedious halts. The Governor and I were morning men, and frequently I would see him and his dog, Bruto, walking through the camp an hour before reveille. The late afternoon sky had cleared as the low sun seeped through the pines, and since I was near the center of the village and we had seen no Indians in the last two hours of the march, I had removed my helmet and mail shirt. Rust was becoming a problem with my armor, and everyone's.

From the north end of the village I could hear the return of Gallegos' patrol. Soto normally sent a mounted patrol to scout five miles forward from our campsite. I got to my feet because there was an unusual amount of shouting and commotion. Gallegos was a wire-tough man ten years older than myself; he was kin to Cabeza de Vaca and it was rumored he had invested his entire fortune in the *entrada.* Soto had appointed him constable, an honor for any man.

Gallegos came galloping up to the hut; there was a smile of pride on his craggy face.

"Tell his Excellency that we have captured seventeen natives, and Ortiz believes one is the daughter of the village *cacique*."

Both he and his mount glistened with sweat in the soft, sand-colored light. In full riding armor he dismounted and waited, and without a word I went to the hut entrance, knowing it was exciting news for the Governor and all of us. We now had an excellent chance to capture a village *cacique* and obtain our just control of the heathens. We desperately needed guides, workers, porters, and women. I myself had been grinding corn and gathering wood. It was five days before the actual *cacique,* named Aguacaleyquen, came into camp. He had attempted to send an imposter, but the hoax was uncovered. The *cacique* said he would provide guides and porters for the release of his daughter, but when that did not happen, Soto held both him and the daughter and continued the march. It seemed that Aguacaleyquen was an important man in a polity that included three or four other villages in our line of march toward Apalachee land.

֍

"Ah, Ortiz, sit. Your brow seems furrowed," Don Carlos said. Juan joined Don Carlos and me as we sat at a small snapping pine fire, and he did look tired.

"A bad day for you?" I asked. During the afternoon, as we marched, we could see hundreds of Indians in the woods around us.

"It is maddening," Juan said. "First they come blowing their flutes in friendship, but of course Soto will not release their *cacique*. Then they come with the blowing of the conch shell threatening to bake or boil us if we don't give up Aguacaleyquen, and of course they get nothing."

"What does the Governor say?" Don Carlos asked.

"He is very patient, and laughs at the threats." Juan put his hand to his face rubbing his eyebrows. "I'm tired of all the talk. Soto says he has seen this same behavior in Panama and elsewhere, and in the end we'll get what we want."

"So why be concerned, if the Governor is not?" I asked. Don Carlos added a piece of wood to the fire, sending a small shower of sparks into the damp night air.

"I have lived with Indians for over ten years. The Governor and many others believe that all Indians are alike. That is not true, as it is not true that all Christians are alike. There is a difference in these people. I feel the hatred in their words and their voices. I see the contempt in their eyes and their movements. They are not afraid; they believe they are superior. Our horses and the armor are all just parts of an evil force. A force they believe their gods will help them defeat."

"No one is superior to us," I said. I have mellowed over the years, but then we all believed the Spanish soldier was the best on earth. It had been so all of our lives, for decades.

"Ranjel is right," Don Carlos added.

Juan Ortiz shrugged. "Yes, but they are fearless and can swarm in with two thousand warriors. They are fighting for their homes and women. What do we have here, maybe fifty cavalry and one hundred foot soldiers?"

We three studied the crackling fire for a time. I had learned to listen well to Juan Ortiz's judgment of the Indians.

"Some of the officers," I said, "have asked the Governor to have

Moscoso come up. It may be a good idea, for it is true there are many out there."

"I've also heard the same from the men," Don Carlos said. "There is less talk now of gold and lack of food, and more of the Indians."

"Are they afraid?" Juan asked.

"No, no, but they realize that the Indians can rush us en masse and perhaps overwhelm our small force."

"Many of these people will fight to the death," Juan said.

☙

In the morning the Governor sent riders ordering Moscoso to double-time the main army forward, and within four days they had joined us. Everyone was relieved, and with the *cacique* and his daughter riding with the Governor, the entire army moved northwest. Hundreds of Indians remained in our shadows, and their threats continued. At one point, they said they would send flocks of birds to drop flesh-eating vermin on us to rot our bodies and poison our food and water. We laughed, but the savages were serious. They believed their *caciques* had control over all of nature's wonders.

I prayed with the Father the next morning.

As the trail turned west the Indians turned more conciliatory and apologized for their threats, and they promised to serve our needs at the next village of Napituca. In fact, they started to provide us with porters, guides, food, and servants. Our spirits were again on the rise.

Napituca was a pleasant village with an ample supply of food, and it was situated adjacent to two spring-fed lakes. The Governor, with me and several officers, moved into the large residence the *cacique* had abandoned.

The next day three painted flute players, followed by a messenger with a fancy feathered headdress and jeweled marten robe, arrived saying that seven area *caciques* had agreed to help us fight the Apalachee if Aguacaleyquen was released. The Governor was friendly as usual, saying that the *cacique* and his daughter were not prisoners. They were just accompanying us to the border with the Apalachee, but he agreed to meet with the other *caciques* who were afraid to enter the village for fear of becoming hostages. A meeting with the *caciques* and Soto was arranged for two days hence on an open savanna outside of the village.

ॐ

"Governor," Moscoso said, "with all honor, I do think you should take more than six men with you. There are still many armed and dangerous savages in the forest." Several officers and I were gathered in the hut with the Governor the morning before his meeting with the *caciques*.

"I agree with the *maestro de campo*," Anasco, the mariner, said. "There is grave risk here and your Excellency is too important to our mission."

"Select one of us to go in your stead," said Lobillo, the young captain from Peru days. A rare breeze came through the open door. Soto raised both hands.

"As a child of the sun," he said, with a rare smile, "I have no fear, and the natives must see and understand that. Of course we all know there is some risk, but we are undertaking a holy mission with a noble goal, and we understand there must be sacrifice. Espindola will have extra halberdiers standing by, but I think these natives understand our superiority and will service us until we reach the Apalachee."

"That is a large field," Lobillo said, "you could be two crossbow shots from Espindola's halberdiers, and the savages are fast."

There was some confusion outside of the hut, and Cristóbal de Espindola, head of Soto's personal guards, stepped inside.

"Ortiz is here. He says it's very important."

"Send him in." Juan came in looking breathless and wild-eyed.

"My three Urriparacoxi interpreters came to me this morning and told of a plot by the Indians to assassinate you at the meeting today and to capture and kill all of us. The interpreters were told if they cooperated, that they would be given beautiful wives and allowed to live here, or they would be safely escorted back to their own country. Uriutina, the local *cacique*, met with them last night, but they came to me this morning." Ortiz's eyes glanced quickly around the room, and a hint of pride crossed his tense face.

"Go on," urged Moscoso. We all were staring at the pale face of Juan Ortiz.

"When the Governor is at the meeting in the field he will be seized and carried off where warriors rushing in will kill him. Meanwhile, other warriors will enter the village and kill or capture all of us. Uriutina believes our men have grown careless and lazy and will be caught off guard. He said our men are weak without armor and horses. All of us will be put to death by roasting, boiling, or hanging upside down in the trees for the birds. Others will be buried to their necks, or fed poison that will slowly rot them away. . . . This is all I know."

"Very good, Ortiz," Soto said. "We shall not disappoint the savages." Soto's head and eyes moved from officer to officer. "We will give the appearance of being careless and lazy, but we will be ready. We can finally fight them in an open area." I could see the gleam in his black, cavalryman's eyes.

"Now here is what we must do. . . ."

•

Cabeza de Vaca was the mysterious man who survived Narváez's failed entrada into La Florida in 1528, and his return to Spain years later had caused considerable excitement about possible riches in the area. Two important leaders of the entrada were kinsmen of de Vaca; they were Baltasar de Gallegos and Cristóbal de Espindola. Both of these men had invested their fortunes in the entrada.

Having a supply of slaves was an important factor for the morale of de Soto's army. Many of the officers and men felt it was beneath them to carry supplies, gather wood, feed animals, cook meals, or perform other similar tasks. After all, they were trained for fighting as conquistadors. In addition, young women were needed. Few of the men had problems with this attitude toward the conquered people, for they believed their cause to be divine and just, granting victors the right to enslave the conquered.

The cacique and his daughter were captured near present-day Lake City, Florida.

Chapter 7

The Governor, taking Aguacaleyquen by the hand, followed two tall native messengers out into the field of short para grasses. The afternoon sun reflected off the natives' red-painted faces and headdresses containing tufts of standing feathers. Juan Ortiz walked with the Governor and the *cacique*. Juan carried the Governor's saddle, which the Governor would use for a chair. They were followed by six of Espindola's finest halberdiers. Playing his role, Soto chatted causally with Aguacaleyquen.

Moscoso and I sat as if playing chess at the rear of a village hut overlooking the grassland. Inside the hut, our horses were saddled and ready for battle. Many of the cavalrymen sat mounted and hidden in the huts, eager and ready to use their lances and swords, for they had had little opportunity to display their field skills since arriving in *La Florida*. The footmen were seemingly working or lounging about, but all were prepared and ready. A trumpet would sound at the first sign of an Indian attack, and the entire army was primed to rush into action.

From the forest on the far side of the plain the other *caciques* and their escorts emerged. The group of twelve walked slowly toward the Governor's party; several wore long, white robes. The shadows of clouds moved mysteriously across the area.

"I don't like this," Moscoso said. "The Governor will be out-numbered two to one." Soto had reached the center of the field and had stopped. Moscoso got to his feet. His lips pressed hard together, his hand signaled me to remain seated.

"I'm going to check the horses," he said. "This is utter madness. If we lose the Governor our quest for gold is gone." He disappeared around the hut.

At the center of the field the two parties were standing in what seemed to be friendly discussion. At two places at the forest's edge I saw individual Indians moving about. Our men had ceased their pretence of leisure and all eyes were on the meeting at the center of the field. Ortiz placed the saddle on the ground and Soto took his seat. From the corner of my eye I saw an Indian leave the forest to uncover his bow and arrows that he had hidden in the grass. Others also appeared.

Moscoso, mounted, came charging around the hut, his lance at the ready, yelling, "At them men, at them! Santiago, Santiago. Go for them, knights. Go for them!" The trumpet sounded, as dozens of Indians were now pouring out of the forest and running toward the Governor. I jumped up, ran into the hut, and leaped onto Boot. I charged down the field with the second wave of cavalry. Ahead I could see that Espindola's men had surrounded the Governor and Ortiz, who were parrying with their swords as the Indians moved in around them. I saw Moscoso run his lance through the chest of a club-wielding native. The move almost took him from his saddle. As he slowed to shake his lance free, a huge native came running at him with his club raised. I arrived in time with my sword to sever the Indian's club-swinging arm at the elbow. His blood bathed my leg as Boot brushed passed, knocking him to the ground.

I charged on toward the Governor, who was being helped onto a horse. He had just mounted when the animal went down with a dozen arrows in its chest and legs. Arrows were coming from all directions; I could feel some hitting my plates. A cavalryman quickly dismounted. Ortiz helped the Governor mount his animal, and Soto charged off to organize the battle effort. For minutes it was a maelstrom of fighting. A native grabbed my leg attempting to pull me off Boot. I decapitated him with a short back thrust; I recall his eyes still wide as the head hit the grass. I needed to sever the man's wrist as his hand remained caught in my leg strap.

The Indians fought well but soon were driven from the field; they had no defense for our speeding and trampling cavalry. Some escaped into the forest, but many were forced to go into the two lakes to elude a certain death. Both lakes were cold, deep, and spring fed, one lake much smaller than the other. As the sun set, Soto ordered that the smaller lake be completely surrounded, trapping over three hundred warriors treading in the center of its chilly water.

We had lost three men with nine wounded in the brief battle, and we buried over forty warriors in a mass grave. Soto remained at the lake's edge during the night, having Ortiz frequently plead for Indians to surrender. We needed them as slaves, but he also did not want to martyr them with a mass drowning.

The long hours of the night dragged by, and fires were built to encourage the frigid natives to come ashore. Just before dawn the exhausted men started to swim in slowly, one or two at a time. They fell to the ground and were helped to the fireside. It had been a noble but futile effort. Shortly after sunrise, Soto ordered our Urriparacoxi slaves to go into the lake to bring the few remaining *caciques* to shore. They went in and pulled them out by their hair. Among them was the leader of the failed ruse, Uriutina.

As the Indians recovered, their wrists were tied behind them and they were taken to a huge lodge in the village. They remained there under heavy guard throughout the day as our army reorganized and rested. It had been a difficult but satisfying victory.

⁊

There were still a few stars fading from a cloudless sky as I walked to the hut where Juan Ortiz had slept. He and several officers were up preparing for the day.

"The Governor," I said, "wants to talk to the chiefs. He still hopes to make peace before heading into Apalachee land." Ortiz looked tired and sat down on his saddle. He gave me a weak smile, shaking his head.

"I don't know about the Indians in Panama or Peru," Juan said, "but from what I gather from the Governor and others they were not like these. Those Indians, after a defeat like yesterday, apparently would give up and become like sheep. These Indians lost yesterday, but today is a different day, a different battle to wage. I know how they think. They will not give up; they will die first. Today is another day, another day of an endless war. The Governor doesn't understand this." Juan put his hand to his brow and closed his eyes.

"What about the commoners, the slaves?" Ayala, the majordomo, asked. Most of the officers and men wanted and needed slaves and porters. Many of the others had escaped or died during the past weeks.

"They will be given out," I said, "to those who have chains."

"Good," Lobillo said, "we've got the chains."

The Governor and Ortiz walked among the prisoners and released the six *caciques*. The Governor suggested they patch up their differences and work together to defeat the feared Apalachee. The *caciques* listened but said little. Earlier, Uriutina, after being pulled from the lake, had asked to send a messenger to his leader, the head *cacique* named Uzachile. Soto discovered that Uriutina had told the messenger to tell Uzachile not to give in to the Spaniards and to continue the fight. Soto would not allow the messenger to leave the village.

During the afternoon the hundreds of captured Indians were distributed among the officers and men as slaves. Most were led off in chains. The new slaves would start carrying and grinding corn, gathering wood, cutting grass for animal feed, and doing whatever work their masters commanded of them. I could see the hate and defiance in their black eyes and on their paint-streaked faces as they were led away.

To show our friendship, the Governor gathered his lead officers together outside his hut to meet with the unchained *caciques*. Without Juan Ortiz, who was at the Governor's side, it was impossible to communicate with the Indian leaders, so from the start it was an awkward gathering. I had been called away for a moment, and when I returned I saw Uriutina, who was seated next to the Governor, jump to his feet, giving a loud, wild, blood-stopping cry. He then reached down and grabbed the Governor by the collar and delivered a viscious blow to Soto's mouth and jaw. The Governor fell over backwards in his chair unconscious. The *cacique* jumped upon him, beating him with his fists. I drew my sword and rushed to his aid, but two of Soto's guards had quickly stepped forward, nearly decapitating the *cacique* with their swords. I help pull the dead and bloody Uriutina off the Governor whose mouth and lips were bloody, blue, and swollen. He had lost two teeth.

Uriutina's outcry touched off a revolt throughout the camp by the captured Indians. They grabbed any loose item they could use as a weapon and attacked their captors. Swords, lances, cooking vessels, and firewood were used. One of our men was killed when beaten by a heavy maize grinding pestle; another was strangled to death by the infidel's own wrist chains, and many more were injured. It was a half an hour before order was restored. Dozens of the slaves were killed.

The Governor was almost unrecognizable with his missing teeth and swollen and distorted mouth. It would be weeks before he could eat properly. When he regained his senses, he ordered all the rebel Indians brought to the main square where some were slaughtered by halberds, but most were tied to posts and shot through with arrows. Most arrows were shot by the Urriparacoxi and other Indians we had captured earlier; they had been ordered to do this. They would not be eager to escape after word got out that they killed their neighbors. Only the young slaves were spared. It took hours as the dozens of bodies were dragged away and the new victims were tied to the posts. Many of us thought that Soto had acted improperly in this wanton butchery. Slaves were needed and the execution of a few would have served the same purpose. The smell of blood blanketed the village for days.

๛

On September 23, 1539, we moved out of Napituca toward the villages of the head *cacique,* Uzachile. These villages were abandoned and the *cacique* was in hiding. At a flooded river, a group of hostile Indians shot arrows at us from the far bank. They had little effect, but Soto's war dog, Bruto, broke loose from the page holding him and plunged into the river. He was trained to kill Indians, and none of our desperate calls could turn him back. We watched as arrows protruded from his head and back, but the huge mastiff staggered onto the far shore before falling dead. The Indians danced around the body before chopping it up and throwing it into the river. The animal's head was left impaled on the end of an upright stick. We trudged forward in search of a suitable winter camp. Our victory at Napituca had been sadly dampened by the natives' revolt and their mass executions.

Ahead, beyond the villages of Uzachile, we would finally encounter the fierce and storied Apalachee.

•

The normally pragmatic de Soto acted out of character following the Battle of Napituca. On his orders, over two hundred Indians were massacred, most tied to stakes and shot with arrows. He had been advised against this type of action by the Council of the Indies before leaving Seville, but, like almost every other leader of the conquistadors, he ignored these orders. He believed, like the other entrada *leaders, that the aging men on the Council did not understand what it took in a raw and violent land to make the natives obey the will of God's chosen people.*

Every member of de Soto's entrada *had heard and discussed Cabeza de Vaca's long and difficult journey out of* La Florida *starting in the summer of 1528. De Vaca had blamed Pánfilo de Narváez, the* entrada *leader, for their defeat in the cane-choked salt marshes of Apalachee Bay. It had been Narváez's mistreatment of the Indians that had led to his clash with the fierce Mississippian tribe of the Apalachee. Nevertheless, many of de Soto's men were eager to meet the Apalachee warriors they had heard so much about. It would be a test of their military skills.*

Chapter 8

Three years ago my son was able to obtain, from the daughter of Gonzalo Oviedo de Valdés, my official notes from the *entrada*. Although damaged by water and time, they are readable. Following the *entrada,* it was weeks after we arrived in Panuco, Mexico, before I was able to return to Havana. It was the fall of 1543. There I was required to turn my journal over to Oviedo, who was the royal historian. I had not seen the notes in those many years. Now I use them daily as I write; they trigger my memories. I apologize for pausing in the narrative, but yesterday at wine hour I studied with my eyeglass three faint words in the margin of the notes: Manzana, bronze, forever. The notes I wrote were, of course, for the Governor's official record. Those three faint words were personal words of mine and have rekindled my aging mind—although, I confess to thinking of the woman Manzana often during the last thirty years.

Three days after leaving Napituca, Gallegos captured two dozen women gathering maize. They were handsome women. The Governor added two to his personal staff and one was assigned to me as cook and servant. Months later we discussed the possibility that Uzachile had arranged their capture as a means of pacifying us as we marched through his country, for the very next day we also received a gift of deer meat from him. We will never know; I renamed my woman Manzana, the Spanish word for apple. We communicated by signs; however, I did have two conversations with her with the help of Juan Ortiz. She was the daughter of a minor *cacique*; she was seventeen years old. Her husband had drowned a month after their marriage, in a fishing boat accident. She would soon be assigned a new husband.

At five feet six inches she was taller than most of the native women, with dark, curly hair falling over her shoulders. She was handsome, with liquid brown eyes, but it was the color and texture of her skin and the flawless form of her body that set her apart. Her body was curving, bronze, and silky; she was the most sensual woman I had ever seen. She wore a white, bleached deer hide skirt and top and thin bleached hide bands around her head and ankles, with a pink shell necklace.

From the moment our eyes met, we both could sense a powerful, formidable attraction. It was more than sexual, a unique alignment of all our senses.

Up until now I have not mentioned the relations between our men and the native women. Men who have been with the military or in gaming tournaments or with other sizable groups of young men for prolonged periods understand, and you mix in captured women and spirits and you often get lustful, disgusting behaviors. There were many of these, and early in the *entrada* I wrote in the notes of my disgust. The Governor told me to remove those pages, saying the official record did not need those details or my personal opinions. I recall him asking, with his clenched smile, if I would write about shoeing my horse or of a difficult bowel moment. I will add that the Governor himself was in no way one of the men I had written about, but he did turn his back and provided the men with women whenever possible. I know the Governor had a few women, but always in private and never without consent.

I talked to Father Castilla about the licentious behaviors; he told me to pray for both the men and women. He had discussed these issues with the Governor long before in Panama, with no result.

Two evenings after Manzana came to us I was rinsing my undershirt in a clear but tannin-colored creek rambling through a mangrove thicket. Manzana came beside me. She waded in to her waist and removed her hide top and scrubbed it with a smooth sandstone rock. After leaving the stream she hung the top on a mangrove limb and removed her skirt. Squatting in knee-deep water she cleaned her skirt. All of these fluid moments she did as if fixing maize at our campsite. I stood like a statue, but I could feel my blood surging.

I can see her as if yesterday, the wet, bronze, Aphrodite body glistening in a fading sun.

Imagination still rules our world; we must all use it when my words fail.

Workmanlike, she came and undressed me, washing and hanging up my garments. I stood frozen in awe and anticipation. Then she led me into the creek. The water was to her breasts; there she scrubbed my body with her hands and the sandstone.

Satisfied that her work was completed, she came to me and smiled, her eyes bright, darting, daring. We kissed with a hunger, her small hands caressing me and my hands gripping her firm buttocks.

I led her to a grassy area among the rushes where we kissed and fondled. We were there for hours; wave after wave of our needs swept us along through a wild and thoughtless bliss.

༁

For the next ten days we marched through the land and villages of the *cacique* Uzachile. The villages were abandoned, and we saw very few natives and nothing of the *cacique*. Travel was easy through the maize fields and around the lakes in the tall pine forests. The pace had been slowed somewhat by the Governor's injury. Every night I met Manzana, and each night was better than the previous one. After all the years I can feel her breath on my neck and ears and the press of her powerful body. I have never again been as free and all-feeling.

I have a fine wife, who has given me four children over the last almost thirty years, but with her and other women I've known it was never the same as with Manzana; perhaps it is the burden that comes with marriage, or the many responsibilities of family and profession, or of the Church, or of age. Each of us carries a certain amount of personal burden, like a roll of belly fat in the mind.

One afternoon after the march, Soto called a meeting of his chief officers. His mouth had mostly healed and he looked nearly normal. He announced that in two days we would near the end of Uzachile's territory, and things would change. First there would be a five-mile thicket, a buffer zone between the feuding tribes. Then we would enter the much-anticipated—and feared—Apalachee territory.

"Remind the men," Soto said, "that all slaves must be chained at night. Those from this region will fear entering Apalachee land and be ripe for escape, and they will all be needed for our winter camp." He looked at several of the officers and me. For the first time I saw a gray hair in his beard. I had not chained Manzana for the last two weeks. I lowered my eyes. I trusted her. How could I put an iron collar on her?

Two nights later Manzana and I lay under tall pines. Clouds raced passed a three-quarter moon, and in the distance we could see heat lighting. She took charge of our joining, having me lie still as she kissed and nibbled over my body. The next day I understood the perfect, magnificent night, for it was our last.

In the morning Manzana was gone. She left a small bunch of tiny white flowers by my pack and a carved pink shell. Juan Ortiz told me the carving in the shell was a symbol that meant "forever." I pressed one of the flowers in the journal and can still see the outline where it had dried and remained for years. I later lost the shell in a native hut fire.

My shock over Manzana's escape was quickly magnified by the fury of the Governor. His face was purple and livid with rage; he pounded the morning table. His own secretary had disobeyed him. Ayala, the majordomo, was ordered to place me in chains and I was to be flogged at the noon halt as an example to all. I later learned that Moscoso, Don Carlos, and Father talked Soto out of the flogging, but I marched two days with the foot soldiers before returning to Boot and my saddle. The Governor and I never spoke of this matter again, but I later realized that for Manzana it was the best thing that could have happened. It is possible that she is still alive today somewhere back in *La Florida*. She would never have survived what we were about to face.

I have written that the Governor was quick to anger and often reacted on impulse. This was true following the escape of Manzana and three other prisoners. Frequently, as the moment cooled he would be talked out of his first unthinking decision. He was then able to erase from his conscious slate the entire event. He did this better than anyone I have ever known. He needed no healing or rehashing or questioning of the affair; it was as if the episode had not occurred. He was a very gifted man in many ways, and the more I was with him the more I recognized his unique character.

The memory of her has been with me daily throughout the many years, a brief but beautiful landmark in my life: Manzana, bronze, forever.

•

I have met with Arturo LaBelle twice in Mexico City concerning Ranjel's original journal and notes. They cannot be found. All that remains is this manuscript written by Ranjel years later from those missing documents. Oviedo, the Royal Historian of the Indies, used Ranjel's notes and also talked with Ranjel. However, experts believe Oviedo added much of his own voice to Ranjel's writing. I have been careful to avoid this in working with this manuscript. What you have are Ranjel's words and my humble translation.

It is difficult to imagine the tough, grueling everyday life of the entrada: the harsh elements, the lack of food, the constant threat of attack and death. We do know from Ranjel's manuscript, as well as from Oviedo's writing, that Ranjel often did not agree with the brutal treatment of women and natives. In this regard, he was different from the majority of officers and men.

Chapter 9

The march turned grueling as we moved west into Apalachee territory. We hacked our way along narrow single-man trails snaking through cane swamps, tangled forests, and over flooded rivers. After surprising the first small Apalachee village, the natives were ready and attacked us at every pinch point. Our horses, crossbows, and harquebuses were ineffective in these cramped quarters, and the warriors' long bows were capable of rapid and deadly fire. But our foot soldiers pushed on, often marching through a sleepless night. Several nights I slept leaning on Boot with water to my knees. The black nights were a noisy, natural hell.

The Apalachee warriors attacked from one side of the narrow trails and then the other. With this pattern they would not be shooting into their own companions. After that first village, all the small villages were abandoned, but there was evidence of an ample food supply. That cheered Soto, for winter was approaching and there were hundreds of mouths to feed. However, the men of the rank and file, hot and wet in their quilted armor, chain mail, and metal jackets, and facing daily attacks, had little to cheer about. And above all else there was no trace or word of gold.

After days, and the loss of four men and several horses, we thankfully broke through the back swamps and proceeded into a pine barren, longleaf pines with a forest floor of wiregrass. The trails widened, but the Apalachee had positioned horizontal log barriers to slow the cavalry, a technique they developed in defeating Narváez.

We broke into open terrain and huge fields of maize ready for harvest. There were also pumpkins, squash, and beans. Here the cavalry caught up with and killed or captured every native seen. Still, the tenacious Apalachee persisted in assaulting our men at every opportunity, and they burned the first large town we came to. Nevertheless, we rested there a day as the food was plentiful.

We were angered by the continual Apalachee boasting that they would kill and destroy all of us as they had the army of Pánfilo de Narváez. There was something about the obstinacy and rancor of these people that was galling. Soto and others were determined to teach them a lesson.

The tenacity of the native women was equal to that of the men. Don Carlos told us of a young officer in his company who took a woman into a cornfield for pleasure. There she grabbed his genitals and he was unable to extricate himself and had to yell for help. Even Soto smiled at the man's embarrassment. The woman was tied wrists to ankles over a fence rail and assaulted by several during the night. In the morning she was still spitting at her attackers; she was later fed to the dogs.

Led by the cavalry, we marched on through fields of maize toward the Apalachee capital of Anhaica. This was their largest and most well-built city, and the natives chose not burn it. Here Soto decided to make our winter camp. There was housing and food for all of our men and animals; we would be there for five months.

The months at the winter camp of 1539–1540 went quickly, but at no time were we ever free from guerrilla attacks by the Apalachee. Several men and animals died, and twice sections of the city were burnt. I was housed with the Governor in the large home of the Apalachee *cacique,* Capafi, built on a high mound.

Soto actually captured the obese chief, but inexplicably he escaped. Juan Ortiz told us that the fat man moved about his house by crawling on all fours; outside he was carried on a litter.

The Governor sent reconnaissance groups in all directions. Stocks of food and any captured natives were brought back to Anhaica. Anasco led a group of cavalry and footmen south to find a trail to the coast. He found a trail to a broad bay where Narvaez had built his ill-fated flatboats. There they found heaps of horse bones, confirming that before sailing the men had eaten their horses. Anasco named it the Bay of the Horses. All of us thought of those desperate men trapped in a strange land between the forbidding sea and the fierce Apalachee.

The Governor had picked some outstanding captains to lead his army, but some he relied upon more than others for difficult assignments. Two of these were Baltasar de Gallegos and Juan de Anasco. Another was my friend Luis de Moscoso, although Soto counted on Moscoso mainly for camp and march management, where he excelled.

A week after returning from the Bay of Horses, Anasco, with thirty cavalrymen, was ordered to ride back to the base camp at Ozita and have those troops join us at Anhaica. One of the ships there would return to Havana and bring Isabel up to date on the *entrada;* the others would sail with the supplies and foot soldiers to the Bay of Horses. It was a dangerous mission.

Anasco made the 320-mile trek in ten days. He traveled over the same hostile route that had taken us three months to cover, with the loss of only two men and two horses. It was a brutal journey, and at the village of Napituca where Soto had been assaulted, Anasco found the village burnt to the ground. The bodies of the natives massacred there were still stacked unburied, food for the birds and wild beasts.

While Anasco was sailing north with the men and supplies and Pedro Calderón led the guard's cavalrymen back up the coast to Anhaica, Soto continued an attempt to pacify the Apalachee. He used every tactic and terror trick he knew to frighten, cajole, and bludgeon them into obedience. There were days of intense and ruthless torture. Many of the native's hands and noses were cut off. Several were burned at the stake, and others were thrown to the dogs. Still they would not relent, and over twenty Spaniards were killed during the five months at Anhaica; many of those were scalped. The skirmishes were incessant.

From the Bay of Horses, Soto sent Francisco Maldonado in Anasco's caravels west to find a suitable harbor. He returned with word of a great river, a native village, and a fine harbor. Maldonado was then ordered to return to Cuba and have supplies there in the fall for Soto and the army.

ॐ

"I think you'll live," Don Carlos said, dabbing the wound with a whisky-soaked rag. Moscoso had a slight wound in his right side from a native arrow. I studied the arrow.

"It's standard cane," I said.

"What galls me," Moscoso said, "is I paid a hundred and fifty ducats for that damn hauberk." The arrow had gone right through his expensive coat of burnished mail, and he could have been seriously wounded if the arrow had hit him straight in.

"I just heard," Juan Ortiz said, hustling up to the hut. "How are you?"

"He's all right," I said. "He's just upset that his fancy mail didn't stop this arrow." I handed the arrow to Juan.

"Ah yes," Juan said, toying with the arrow as he gave Moscoso a pat on the shoulder. "The day before yesterday, one of Gallegos' men put a coat of mail like yours over an empty wine barrel and a native shot a plain cane arrow through the front and out the back."

"I'm sure it wasn't as fancy a coat as Luis'," Don Carlos said.

"A blanket coat is better than this piece of dung," Moscoso said, fingering the mail coat on his lap.

"Listen up, friends," Juan said. "I have news, good news at last. Yesterday Gallegos' men brought in a young prisoner named Perico, who came here with a trading party from the north. He is from a province called Cofitachequi, ruled by a woman. It's about two weeks' march northeast, and has much gold, silver, and many pearls." You could hear only a distant crow as we stared into Juan's huge dark eyes; this might be the answer to our prayers.

"Why," Moscoso asked, "should we believe some strange youth?"

"He knows how gold is mined, melted, and refined."

A jolt ran through us; the entire army would again be confident that God and Hernando de Soto would lead us all to great personal wealth.

The Governor planned to march in a great arch to the north and east, plunder Cofitachequi, and return south and meet Maldonado for supplies in the fall.

•

Experts are still debating the exact route that de Soto took during much of his invasion of the Southeast; however, they do agree on where he wintered in 1539–40. It was in what is now downtown Tallahassee, about a half a mile from the State Capitol building. Archaeologists have found several items at the site, including clumps of iron chain mail.

Readers must also keep in mind that the topography that Ranjel witnessed was far different from that seen today. Over half of the state of Florida was forested wetlands; today only about ten percent is. Except for a few small spots in southern Georgia, the longleaf pine–wiregrass forests are gone. The fruits, berries, and nuts, as well as the animals, fish, and birds, have all changed to varying degrees. For example, the main Apalachee animal fat was bear oil.

The appearance of the youth named Perico was significant for de Soto. After three hard, weary months of travel and no gold, morale was low. The De Soto Chronicles, two excellent volumes written in 1993, report that when Anasco reached the base camp at Ozita the men there did not first ask about their friends but about gold. With these conditions it didn't take much to once again fire up the men's greed for gold; Perico provided the spark.

De Soto's plans were to meet Maldonado in either what is Pensacola Bay or Mobile Bay, most likely Mobile Bay. In fact no one from the outside world would see any of de Soto's army for over three years.

Chapter 10

On the third of March, 1540, the Governor led our gold-dreaming army north out of Anhaica. Every man was loaded with maize, for we knew it would be days before we came to the first village. We were forced to carry our own food as most of our porters had died during the winter. Looking back, I cannot understand how we allowed hundreds of slaves to become almost a perishable commodity, but most mornings during that winter I would see the bodies of natives being dragged off for burial in mass graves. These Indians had died of overwork, malnutrition, fatigue, and despair, with heavy iron chains chafing their necks, wrists, and ankles. They were forced to sleep on bare, wet, and frigid ground, with minimal food and clothing. Add disease, and there is little wonder that most succumbed. It is sad to recall.

Except for stretches of pine forest, the travel north was testing for all of us. There were numerous cypress ponds, swamps, and flooded rivers to cross. We spent nights bogged down in alligator- and snake-infested marsh areas fighting off clouds of mosquitoes. The first natives we encountered killed five men from Soto's personal guard. The tiny swamp villages we encountered were poor and backward with little food, so we trudged on. Finally after we made a difficult passage over the flooded Flint River, we came to the village of Toa; this town was part of a new, more advanced polity. The natives here were much more sophisticated, unafraid, and surprisingly direct and congenial. The men and officers were pleased.

Here Soto was again convinced that he was nearing a great and wealthy kingdom. He wanted to push on without staying the day, but some of the exhausted foot soldiers would not budge. This resistance came not from the *hidalgos* but the commoners and mercenaries. At times like these the Governor told me he wished he were not encumbered by such an army. He preferred to command small, highly mobile squads of cavalry.

With scenes of Inca gold in his mind, the Governor could not be restrained. He was up at midnight ordering me and his forty best horsemen to prepare to ride. We rode hard for thirty-six hours into a neighboring kingdom named Ichisi. Here the people crowded around us in a festive manner. I had seen nothing like it, but for Soto it recalled his early days of the Inca campaign. The food was good and we rested there the following day as Soto tried to learn more about the journey to Cofitachequi, but we found no Indians that had actually been that far north.

That afternoon the king of Ichisi, an affable, one-eyed man wearing a long, red, woven robe, came to Soto, saying he had women for him and each man of his vanguard. The Governor attempted to decline the offer, but it was apparent that the king would be offended if it was not accepted. The Governor wanted no trouble.

"Ranjel," Soto said, with a rare, missing-tooth smile, "tell the men to graciously accept their woman. If she does not suit them, so be it, just pat her ass and thank her, but hear this, I don't want any of these women mistreated."

Most men were elated, and I heard of no mistreatment. There would be other similar offers in the future; however, I do clearly recall my woman from Ichisi. She was not Manzana, but she was friendly, ample, and skilled in the pleasures.

We continued northward through the friendly villages of Atamaha, Ocute, and Cofaqui. At Cofaqui we were at the northern edge of the territory of the gracious Ichisi tribes. Here we faced a buffer zone of an uninhabited and mountainous wilderness. The Ichisi hated and feared the Cofitachequi, but we Spanish were eager to get on to this land of rumored great treasure.

In Cofaqui a difference of opinion surfaced between the boy-guide Perico and the Ichisi natives. Perico claimed the wilderness area could be crossed in four days; the natives said at least ten days would be needed. Soto warned Perico he had better be right, for the youth had advanced to almost *hidalgo* status among the officers. The Ichisi agreed to go with us to help fight their enemy the Cofitachequi, and they knew of a fishing trail that went about halfway, ending at a great river. Thus we set off with over seven hundred native warriors and porters. We followed the fishing trail for four days through a mountainous forest of oak, hickory, and loblolly pine.

Two days later at the wide, flooded river where the Ichisi fished, the trail abruptly ended. It was apparent that Perico did not know the way to Cofitachequi nor did any Ichisi. Soto was furious and ordered Perico thrown to the dogs.

He was stripped and pleaded on his knees; the dogs were straining at their leashes before Juan Ortiz and Father convinced Soto to spare the youth. Later Soto told me the only reason he spared Perico was he was a vital link in Ortiz's complex interpreter chain. However, Perico was put in chains; his days of privilege had ended.

With a short food supply, Soto ordered the Ichisi to return to their villages; meanwhile, a hungry and unhappy army cut their way through swamps and thickets, moving slowly without clear direction. Soto led a scouting party forward, but he returned to camp disheartened. The next day he called a meeting of his captains.

There was talk of turning back, but Soto quickly squelched those thoughts. In time of crises, the Governor had a way of being in control and optimistic. We needed the will to persevere and when he claimed we would, we believed him. He organized four search parties with his best captains, strongest men, and ablest horses. Before the patrols left, he had some of the three hundred pigs killed so each man would have a pound of meat.

At the hungry main camp rain fell and the time dragged as we waited and hoped. Soto was always testy during these times. After a long wait of three days, Anasco's exhausted platoon staggered back to camp. He had found a small village called Himahi some twenty miles to the southeast with a fair supply of corn and flour. Leaving notes for the other patrols still out, the army headed for Himahi. We needed to move with haste, for the men and animals were starving. Some reached the village that night, but many more, exhausted, lay scattered along the trail miles from the town. Food was taken to them and they staggered in the next day.

Meanwhile five Indian men were captured and brought to Soto. He tried to coerce them into guiding us to Cofitachequi. They refused, and he had one burnt alive at the stake. I vividly recall this gruesome day, for all five were burnt one by one. None would lead the way, and for two days the smell of their burning flesh hung over the village. It is an oily, pungent smell, different from a crematorium.

The very next day Gallegos arrived with a woman who was willing to lead us north to Cofitachequi. With plundered food and a willing guide, excitement again gripped the men. Perhaps the Governor was right about *La Florida*. We traveled north through pleasant rolling hills of hardwoods and pine.

At the edge of a medium-size but flooded river we watched a dozen large canoes push off from the far bank and head toward us. It was the first of May. At the stern of the lead canoe in a long, white robe and under an awning sat the queen of Cofitachequi. She sat on a colorful mat and two red cushions. Once ashore she welcomed Soto with gifts of blankets and skins. She was a stately woman of Soto's age, and both leaders exchanged kind welcoming words, using the combination of Juan Ortiz and Perico as their interpreting chain.

When the initial words were finished, the queen stepped forward and removed a triple rope of huge pearls from her neck and put them over Soto's head. Soto was greatly touched by this pleasantry and removed from his hand a gold ring with a ruby inset and placed it on the queen's finger. Father later told me the Governor did the same thing in Peru. All was going well.

The queen then asked an elderly man to step forward and address Soto. He told us that this section of the kingdom had recently undergone a catastrophic plague and was struggling to recover. Able men and women were in short supply as was food. The situation was better in their towns to the north. He asked for our understanding.

The main town where the queen resided had over three hundred houses; her palace and a huge temple were in the center of the village each built on a high mound. The natives seemed friendly, and two days later Soto ordered Gallegos to take the main army northeast to a town named Ilapi, where there was much more food. Some thirty of us stayed in Cofitachequi. Soto wanted to determine the treasures of the kingdom, so we remained there for eleven days. While the queen ruled a large area, we were not certain how strong her current control was over its many parts. As in Europe these powers waxed and waned according to conditions such as the recent plague.

Soto was ecstatic when the queen told him she could bring him yellow and white metals, but it would take a few days. Perhaps Perico was right about gold and silver in the kingdom. In a few days the metal started to arrive; the yellow metal was copper and the white metal was slabs of mica. Once again, disappointment.

Soto, of course, remained optimistic, reminding us of the pearls. The problem with the pearls was that they became dark when the natives removed them from the oysters by using fire, and they were further flawed by having holes drilled in them.

Nevertheless, Soto convinced the queen that he and I should go to the main temple and collect pearls from the dead. I never did understand how he did that, although I know that he and the queen were intimate. The queen probably also understood that if she didn't permit gathering the pearls that he would do it anyway.

I consider the temple at Cofitachequi the most beautiful building that I saw in all of *La Florida*. The large building stood on a high mount well over an acre in size. It had high walls with a steep roof covered with mother of pearl. To enter you climbed twenty thirty-foot-long steps to a broad stone walk leading to two enormous wooden doors.

Just inside the doors stood twelve giant sentries carved in

wood, six on each side. These fierce warriors were armed with an array of weapons carved from wood and embellished with mica, copper, pearls, antlers, and shells. In the high main cathedral there were rows of benches holding chests with the remains of royal family members; portraits of the deceased were painted on the covers. The floors were covered with gorgeous mats, and walls were adorned with finely woven decorated wallpaper. To each side were four marvelous rooms stacked high with weapons of every kind. Throughout, there was a faint smell of mold and musk.

Soto and I spent three days in the dark, dusty temple poking among the clothes and bones of the dead. We collected hundreds of pearls. My memory of those days working in the temple is eerie and hazy, but there is no more I care to write. What can I say? I never understood why the Governor picked me for this task.

•

It is interesting to recall that while de Soto was traveling through what is now the southeastern United States, Francisco Coronado was traveling through what is now the southwestern United States. Some of Coronado's men reached the Grand Canyon and beyond.

After leaving the Tallahassee area in the spring of 1540, the army traveled across Georgia, passing near what is now Macon and near Columbia, South Carolina. De Soto met the queen of Cofitachequi near the town of Camden in South Carolina.

Many of the Indian tribes that de Soto encountered, including the Cofitachequi, had completely disappeared within one hundred years following his visit. This was mainly due to the impact of Old World diseases such as smallpox, measles, and flu.

Chapter 11

On the misty morning of May 12, I mounted my restored and able Boot and with the army left Cofitachequi; many were disappointed. It was not because there was no gold or silver found, only damaged pearls. No, it was because many of the men thought this was an excellent place to establish a colony. Establishing a colony, after all, was one of the *entrada* goals, and we had traveled a year and found no better place. The natives were friendly, the soil was good for crops, and we were near the coast and could establish a port. Soto listened to all these views from both his men and officers, and for a brief moment I thought he might agree with them. However, he had already heard tales of another great king ahead in a country called Chiaha, and his mind was set. We could always come back, he said; besides, we must move on so we could meet with Maldonado in the fall. As Moscoso liked to say, the Governor was a man "hard and dry of words," and once he spoke his mind no one would step forward to question him. An unhappy army moved northwest. It was now clear to me that our leader was an explorer first, with above all else an eye for gold.

The discussions of a colony made one pause, for we had traveled a year without a hint of gold, and several older men were beginning to think the best chance for wealth was by acquiring and developing land. Nevertheless, we all prepared to move out.

Just before leaving, however, some of our brutish men riled

the natives into a fight by rummaging through their houses. The queen was infuriated, and Soto discovered that she was planning to run into hiding. Despite what she had done for us, he put her under arrest. She would remain under guard for several weeks as we progressed through her kingdom. She was allowed to keep her servants and handle daily matters of state.

I also discovered that the queen had found a young lover in our Spanish ranks. It seemed strange to me then, a foot soldier and the queen, but now I understand that there is a sexual web weaving through all human activities; war and exploration are no exceptions.

For the next two weeks we moved west through a beautiful range of mountains. After a few days, however, the magnificent views were lost to our minds' eye by the difficulty of the climb and the sudden lack of food. To Soto and others from his Peru days the mountains reminded them of gold and silver country. In fact, one nugget was found in a small stream, but we were in no condition to stop long and investigate. As we staggered from the mountains, the horses were so weak they could not carry the men. Boot was in better shape as I found food for him each night, mostly tree leaves, and I walked with him much of the time.

It was here the queen and her attendants, pretending to attend to a call of nature, disappeared into the forest. We were nearing the edge of her kingdom, and she was fearful that she would not be released. Soto chose not to pursue her as he had already contacted the *cacique* of Chiaha, who had an ample store of maize and was bringing some forward for the famished men and animals.

During our stay in Cofitachequi four men had deserted to live with native women; this is always a problem with occupying forces.

When Soto was told that two more had deserted to pan for gold in the mountains, he sent a squad back for them. The unfortunate men were found and returned to camp; within hours they were tried and sentenced to death by hanging. They were hanged that afternoon, sending a chill through the mustered army forced to watch. Soto's message got through; I recall no further desertions.

We rested for three weeks in Chiaha, where the native food was the best we had experienced. I tasted the first honey I had had since leaving Spain. The natives were friendly at first, playing games and swimming with the men, but after ten days our men had regained their strength and, I should add, their libido. To placate them, Soto demanded thirty women from the *cacique*. The natives were outraged and the following day abandoned their villages. In the end Soto backed off on his demand for the women, for we desperately needed porters when we continued south.

The Governor did not want a war, for the army was just getting its strength back to move on to the next great kingdom. The kingdom we had heard about was known as the House of Coosa. It seems Chiaha paid tribute to the House of Coosa. The paramount chief of Coosa controlled a huge area and was located many days' ride to our south. Once again Soto's foot was itching.

⌇

Don Carlos and I watched as Moscoso's men roughly placed chains and collars on the *cacique* of Coste and fourteen of his principal men. We had traveled three days from Chiaha and were camped outside the village of Coste.

"What happened?" I asked Don Carlos. He had been with Soto

and a small group of men when they entered the village well in advance of the main army.

"The chief and his leaders greeted us outside of town and we walked in with everyone talking and friendly. There was nothing unusual happening. The chief agreed to supply maize and a few porters. As this talk was going on some of our men went looking for maize and started plundering the chief's private supply, and then went rummaging through some of the nearby houses. It was a dumb thing to do, but you know we've got some men who aren't the brightest of candles." Don Carlos gave me his boyish smile.

"Suddenly we're surrounded by at least fifty armed and shouting warriors, dragging our men. The chief is outraged by our men's actions. Believe me, we were in serious danger. Juan will tell you the same thing. They could have killed us all in an instant. Soto stepped forward, yelling at our men as if angry at them but telling them to play his game as he shoves and slaps them. He also told one of his bodyguards to go back and have a squad of armed men move forward quietly one by one. In a short time, Soto had everyone settled down and he apologized to the chief. After he chatted awhile, he took the chief by the hand and walked back toward our camp. The chief's principal men came along with us as we walked. When we got to camp Soto ordered Moscoso to chain and collar all of them.

"When the *cacique* and his men were chained and collared, Soto, who had gone to his tent, emerged in full uniform, helmet, and sword. With Juan Ortiz and his crew at his side he told the *cacique* and his men if they or any of their people were to lay a hand on a Christian again they would be burnt at the stake."

There was no further trouble at Coste, but it was only when we left three days later that the *cacique* and his men were unchained. It was a lesson they would not soon forget, and the story followed us to the House of Coosa.

⚐

As we moved south, the march settled into a pleasant routine that we had not seen before. We had not been attacked in weeks, we had plenty of maize and other foods for the men and animals, and there was an ample supply of male porters and older women as servants. Dozens of young, supple women served as concubines and could easily be bartered for, for pleasures.

Even Soto appeared to relax, if that was possible. One evening he came to me as I was penning my daily entry.

"Not much for the journal these days," he said, sitting on a large log with me.

"I try to give an indication of our daily location and line of march."

"Good . . . a time such as this is good for the men, but it soon, like eating pudding, is over spent."

"They are enjoying it."

"Indeed, but an army is like an individual. Too much of the easy life weakens us."

"It's been a tough year."

The Governor turned and gave me his clenched-jaw smile. He was wearing a black silk robe that Isabel had given him. Over the sash he wore a ceremonial sword he seldom used. It had a jeweled grip and had the following words etched on the blade near the handle: "Do not draw me without reason; do not sheathe me without honor."

I had not seen the Governor outside his tent not wearing his cavalry clothing. He was not a man comfortable with leisure.

"With time, a casual and relaxed march such as this weakens the men and mounts and provides temptation to our enemies."

"The natives are friendly," I said, closing my journal.

"They are friendly because they fear us. If you and I were here alone we would likely be enslaved or burnt at the stake."

I turned and looked into his coal-black eyes; his lips were together and pulled back taut over his teeth. It was that cold granite look.

"Ranjel, if you learn anything from me, let it be this: the one fundamental human motivator is fear. Fear is the key to power, to absolute power. However," he paused and smiled, "power and leadership are not brothers joined at the belly; you can have one without the other. Leadership, first, is making fast and sound decisions in crisis, but perhaps as important is setting goals and having a plan to achieve them." We talked about much more that night, but that is what I recall from over the years. I thought I was beginning to understand the Governor.

უ

We were about a mile from the capital city of Coosa when I first saw the kingdom's sovereign. The twenty-six-year-old king was coming to greet us, being shouldered on a large carrying chair by at least seventy of his principal men. Despite the warm muggy day, the young monarch sat covered by a white robe of marten skins and wearing a tall, feathered headdress. His many carriers were continually being ceremoniously exchanged to the sound of dancing, feathered flute players. We followed the king into the city, which had been cleared for us. After we were given food and entertainment, we were welcomed by several lengthy speeches.

It was here that the Governor exhibited his unorthodox leadership, for he did not step forward and thank the king for his greeting and hospitality. He ordered a prepared and waiting Moscoso to take the king and his men prisoners and put them in chains. He then demanded food, porters, servants, and women from the startled and humiliated young man. The move had surprised me and several of our officers.

During the next few days hundreds of natives were dragged into town, chained, and distributed among our men as slaves. Soto was in complete control.

My friends and I discussed this tactic at some length; there were many pros and cons spoken. I didn't like it nor understand it, but Moscoso agreed with it. He thought the natives were getting too cozy, and there must be no question who is master. Still, it was against my nature, and it left me with an uneasy feeling about our future in this far-off land.

Once more none of us moved about without our swords. Fear brings mastery, but it fosters hate.

•

Most of the native societies that were encountered by de Soto and his army were matrilineal. This means that a person traced his blood relatives only through his mother and female relatives. A person's father was not a blood ancestor, and he was not a male authority figure in one's life; that role fell to the mother's brother. It does not appear that the Spaniards understood or cared about this strange relationship.

Here we see more evidence that forming a colony was not a top priority of de Soto. However, experts believe that he was planning to establish a port on the southern coast, and then set up an inland colony to supply food and labor.

The Coosa capital is believed to have been located near present-day Rome, Georgia.

Chapter 12

With the young king of Coosa, his sister, and his principal men in chains, we moved south through his large, established kingdom. Our men and animals were rested, and we traveled well with the largest group of porters, slaves, and women we had had since arriving in *La Florida*. The caravan stretched for miles. Soto's strategy was working well. At the principal cities the local *cacique*, after a token show of force, was directed by the king to lay down his arms and give us what we demanded.

For a month we traveled easily down broad trails along the eastern side of the Coosa River. Due to the unavailability of food, we moved more rapidly through unpopulated areas. We would soon be approaching the end of the territory of the House of Coosa, and for weeks we had heard much about the fierce Atahachi kingdom we would next enter on our way south to meet with Maldonado on the Bay Ochuse. We had encountered no true resistance since leaving the Apalachee months before. Our only problem had been lack of food.

※

Up to this point in my narrative, I have earnestly followed my journal notes, but we are approaching a critical point of the *entrada*. This is true for the Governor and all of us. It would be three years before I returned to Cuba with my journal, but events of the coming weeks would alter everything. Our physical, mental, and spiritual well-being would forever change, as would our attitude. I now understand that our lives are controlled by many factors, but these factors are all appendages of one's attitude of mind.

I mention this now, for while I will still use my journal, I will be leaning more on my memory and my lengthy discussions with others about these coming events. These discussions took place years later here in the City of Mexico. It was here where several old *entrada* comrades lived and visited with me over the years. With many of these friends, as with me, these events were etched in our memories. Time does not alter nor cloud experiences such as these, and fortunately I have always been a man who made serious notes following these discussions. It has served me well.

༄

One of my dear comrades who now lives near me in the City of Mexico is Luis de Moscoso. He told me of a meeting he had with the Governor during this period in a Tuasi village. I relate it here:

Moscoso had not talked to the Governor in three days; it had become the most leisurely march since our arrival in *La Florida*. As he climbed the twelve-foot-wide stone stairway to the *cacique's* house on a half-acre mound where the Governor was staying, he anticipated why the Governor had asked to speak with him. He had been with the Governor since Peru days, and he understood and admired the man's mode of operating. The Governor was Moscoso's mentor, and he was confident that Soto would want an appraisal of the morale and condition of the troops. Soto understood that

Moscoso was well liked and respected throughout the *entrada* by both officers and men.

Two of Espindola's men with eight-foot-long halberdiers stood on each side of the door to the large, thatched-roofed house. They nodded as Moscoso touched his peaked helmet and entered. The huge main room, where Soto sat, was lit by two sets of seven candles each that he transported with him. Several other smaller rooms were walled off around the perimeter of the central room. The Governor sat at his command table and was talking to the *cacique* using Juan Ortiz and three of his interpreting crew. During the past year Ortiz had developed a group of native men and women for interpreting, for each kingdom the *entrada* passed through had a different language. Ortiz was always searching for natives that spoke more than one language. As the army entered a new kingdom he would patch together the best and shortest chain to get from the local dialect back to Spanish. We all found humor in watching this process, often involving over half a dozen people, but Juan Ortiz took it very seriously, as did the Governor. Good information was vital, and we all knew it. We often discussed what the Governor would have done without Juan Ortiz. It would have been difficult.

The Governor glanced at Moscoso, and signaled with his hand for his captain to have a seat. Moscoso found a stool and took a seat at the far end of the table; he removed his helmet. He smiled at his friend Juan Ortiz. In camp Ortiz was often with the Governor more than anyone, even me.

Moscoso gathered that Soto was trying to get information about the next kingdom to the south from the *cacique's*. The *cacique* had been near there only once in his life, two years before. This kingdom, Atahachi, was still well over one hundred miles to the south. At present the Coosa people were not at war with this fierce neighboring kingdom. The Atahachi king was alleged to be a giant of a man. This *cacique* had met his son, who was also very tall. It took some time to get out this information, but the Governor and Ortiz had developed patience, for they had done this countless times. At one point the *cacique* jumped to his feet, stretching his hand high above his head, hopping up and down. Ortiz explained that this was to show the height of the Atahachi king's son.

Finally the Governor dismissed the *cacique* and Ortiz and his crew, and he told one of his pages to bring in two pewter goblets and the *cacique's* gift flagon.

"Unfortunately the man is stupid," the Governor said, "but Ortiz said that his wine was better than most we've drunk here." Soto motioned at the stool across from him and Moscoso moved up. The Governor had put on a little weight and seemed more relaxed to all of us; it had been a long year for everyone. The Governor poured a dark liquid into the goblets and handed one to Moscoso.

"To God and Spain," Soto said, taking a sip of the liquid.

"And to you, Excellency," Moscoso said, raising his cup. Soto nodded.

"Maldonado will have some decent wine," Soto said, wincing. He drank some more and shrugged his shoulders. "This must do for now. . . . How are the men and horses?"

"The last few weeks have put a snap back in their step, and there is again talk of gold in our future," Moscoso replied.

Soto's lips pulled straight back as his smiling black eyes bore into Moscoso.

"Good, all we need is perseverance and faith and we will find treasure in this land, but I must resupply, and send word and pearls to Cuba, and most importantly, prepare for winter. We know that the coast of Ochuse where our ships will be has few natives and little food. The main army must return inland to winter. It is always a concern, with a group this size."

"Will you establish a post on the coast?"

Soto's eyes narrowed. Moscoso knew Soto did not like answering questions, but this seemed innocent enough.

"A token one only, for shipping. If we find a good wintering site inland we will establish a settlement. Father Castilla is eager to start his work with the natives, and we have men who are land hungry." Soto poured more wine; Moscoso recalled admiring our commander's heavy ruby ring and gold wrist bands that Isabel had given him.

"Starting a colony would allow you a smaller force to search for gold," Moscoso said. This time Soto's lips parted as he smiled. His dark eyes surveyed Moscoso.

"You think well, Luis de Moscoso," Soto said, standing.

Moscoso stood also. He knew his time was up, but he felt good and it wasn't the wine.

As Moscoso turned for the door, Soto asked, "Have you a woman?"

"Yes, Excellency."

"It is good." Soto nodded his approval.

Both Moscoso and I understood that a leader takes care of the needs of his officers.

•

De Soto was a skilled and fearless cavalry officer trained under brutal men like Pedrarias Davila and Francisco Pizarro. He managed without close council, but his men admired him, for he charged into battle without fear or self-regard. Luis de Moscoso was one of the officers as close to him as any.

Ranjel lived in Mexico City after the entrada, *as did several other* entrada *members. These men met with Ranjel over the years, and now we are seeing the first results of these conversations—such that Ranjel could relate scenes where he was not present.*

The northern territory of the House of Coosa was most likely located on the Coosawattee River near the present-day town of Carters, Georgia.

Chapter 13

At the village of Talisi we had reached the southern boundary of the House of Coosa. Soto released the young king, but would not release his sister. I'm not sure why he held the woman, for I'm certain there was no relationship between them. The young king wept on leaving her, for she was a key person in the control of his empire. At the time I thought little about this, but over the years I have thought of this young king and others that we treated in a similar manner. It had to be very difficult to return and face his people; after all, they believed their king to be the invincible, all powerful son of the sun. His people now had seen him in chains and humiliated as hundreds of his people were forced into slavery. We had leisurely marched through his kingdom, taking his food and women and forcing hundreds of men into degrading labor. They carried our supplies, gathered food for our animals, even polished our boots.

Perhaps if I live long enough I will hear how Coosa has changed in the last twenty years, for as I write there is a report that a Spanish explorer named Mateo del Sauz has recently returned to Cuba from a march through Coosa. I hope there was someone in his party who can write, and that we will someday get a report.

We were in Talisi for over two weeks and while there a delegation sent by Tascalusa, the formidable king of Atahachi, arrived. One of the emissaries was the king's eighteen-year-old son. The young man towered over all of us and carried himself with an uncommonly regal bearing. We had heard many stories of the size and fierceness of his father, Tascalusa. There were also rumors from Indian informers that the "giant" king could be planning a surprise attack.

With all this in mind, Soto greeted the prince and his emissaries with a well-staged show of our Spanish might. With trumpets blaring, a group of thirty armored cavalry with swords and lances flashing charged back and forth within yards of the seated ambassadors. All of this was more to instill fear than for ceremonial purpose. The prince and his men sat aloof, even as the swirling dust from the horses wafted over them. Tascalusa had chosen these men with care.

It was agreed that Soto would meet with Tascalusa at his capital city of Atahachi, which was still many miles to the south. According to the native ambassadors there were two different routes to their capital city and they thought it best if we chose the one most suited to our needs. Soto agreed with them; he could rest the army and gather information on this storied kingdom. Thus, for the first time since arriving in *La Florida,* Soto sent two of our Christian men in advance of the army. He selected the respected thirty-six-year-old veteran Diego de Godoy as one of the men. Moscoso and I were with the Governor when he met with Godoy.

"In a few days," Soto said, "we will be going into the kingdom of Atahachi. As you know, stories of all kinds are out there about these people and their king. I have agreed to meet with the king at their capital city, also named Atahachi. Their delegation has told us there are two possible routes to this city. They have suggested that we send a delegation that can determine which route is best for our needs. I suspect that this is just a ruse to give the king and his leaders a chance to inspect some of our force. Therefore, I plan to send only two scouts. There will be no officers or cavalry. These scouts will accompany the prince back to Atahachi."

Soto's black eyes were on Godoy. "My captains have recommended you as our lead scout."

"I would be happy to serve, Excellency. Who goes with me?"

Soto's head and eyes turned turned to Moscoso, who said, "One of the Governor's pages has been working for months with Juan Ortiz. He is the best Christian, besides Ortiz, we have with their languages. We must see and hear all we can."

"Is that Alonso Arias?" Godoy asked.

"Is he a problem?"

"No indeed," Godoy said, "he's a smart young man; he's tough, too." I recalled that Godoy had bested Arias at arm wrestling, but it was a difficult match.

"Good. It is set," Soto said, standing. Everyone stood.

"Find the best trail, but see and hear. I need to know if these people will be a problem. Captain Moscoso will help you prepare."

Godoy, Moscoso, and I walked across the plaza toward where Godoy camped outside of the village.

"The Governor thinks," Moscoso said, "that most of the talk about Atahachi is, in his words, 'a mount of sheep dung,' but I'm not so sure. Juan Ortiz has talked to a lot of natives and he feels that something is going on down there. I was in favor of sending a small force back with them, but the Governor thinks that is what they want, a parade of our men, horses, and weapons, so he won't do it. He saw that his cavalry show did not impress them, so we are now planning to push on through their kingdom as before and take our just Christian rewards. We did convince him to send a couple trail scouts on this mission—of course, that's where you and Arias come in. You two each take a good horse, pack light, and find out what you can. The Governor is likely right—they're just another tribe like the Coosa."

●

Talisi was the southernmost town under the sway of Coosa. It is near the present-day town of Childersburg, Alabama.

De Soto's forces were in Coosa territory for over one hundred days, and after they left this empire was changed forever. Just twenty years later a Spanish force going through the area nearly starved; there were few people and little food. By the 1670s, this Mississippian civilization had disappeared completely.

What caused this disintegration can only be speculated, but certainly diseases carried in by the Europeans were a factor. Starvation could have been involved, as the army took most of the food with winter coming on; in addition, hundreds of the most able young men and women died in slavery. A weakened king could do little to defend his empire.

The enduring effect of the Spanish invasion on these native civilizations was devastating; within a century they disappeared from the continent.

Chapter 14

Diego de Godoy and Alonso Arias, a rugged and gifted youth and future cavalryman, returned to camp in one week. Godoy met with nine of us gathered at the Governor's command table to hear his report.

They had traveled through a country of widely scattered huts and fields of maize, and they had seen very few young men of warrior age. When they asked about this they were told that all the young men had gathered to play in the annual harvest games near the capital city of Atahachi. Godoy had asked permission but had not been allowed to proceed forward to watch the games or go to capital city and meet with Tascalusa.

"In short, Excellency," Godoy concluded after his brief report, "we saw or heard nothing rock-solid suspicious. However, I have a knot in my gut. . . . Things are not as they should be in Atahachi."

We sat staring at Godoy; his report had been simple and direct, but it had ended with this odd warning.

"You and Arias have done well," Soto said, "and I thank you both."

Soto's head and eyes rotated around the table, searching for comments; there were none. He then held his hands up in a priestly fashion as if saying "you have all heard the report."

"With Godoy's caution in your minds, go and prepare. We move out in the morning." We stood and filed out of the large room.

I walked into the plaza with Moscoso, Juan Ortiz, and the veteran captain Baltasar de Gallegos. He was a grizzly and fearless soldier and close to the Governor.

"I hope the Governor was listening to Godoy," Ortiz said.

"He has been busy," I said, "on the report he will send to Cuba with Maldonado. He will send it with the pearls and several slaves for Isabel."

"I know," Moscoso said, shaking his head, "but it is many, many miles before we reach the coast. I agree with Juan. When Godoy has a gut feel about the Atahachi we'd do well to heed it. Besides, this army hasn't drawn a sword in months. Too many men have forgotten the Apalachee warriors and think only of the next cup of that damn black wine . . . or the inviting crease of a woman's ass."

"Ah boys . . . boys," Gallegos said, his voice whiskey-hoarse, "trust the Governor. He has the best instincts and experience of all of us. Right? Listen up, the Coosa and these Atahachi bastards are like blood cousins. True? We'll find them all grapes off the same vine."

As Gallegos turned to go he slapped Moscoso on the back and said, "And these grapes are ready for our picking."

Moscoso shrugged as the three of us watched Gallegos walk off chuckling, his powerful shoulders squared and his sword swinging at his side.

"I hope he's right," Moscoso said. Ortiz rolled his eyes skyward and slowly shook his head.

"I thought with age men become more cautious," I said. My two companions studied me.

"I don't think," Moscoso said, "age is the latchkey here. There are many young and old thinking the same, or more likely not thinking at all. It's a fog that creeps in. It will lift when the first arrows strike."

"Let's hope arrows aren't needed," Ortiz said, "but I see more than fog, and it won't lift quickly. It is like failing to see the flooded river from the canebrake."

༈

The leaves were changing to gold and red, and the air turned cooler as we marched south into Atahachi. The line of the swollen army stretched for many miles, and despite Moscoso's efforts it was difficult to tighten the ranks. In truth, only the Governor could do that, and he was riding up at the front with his personal guard and a few officers. Flags and pennants flapped in the breeze. Directly behind Soto came the most valued supplies and a regiment of cavalry.

Tascalusa had sent the young prince back as a personal guide. In addition to his servants, he was accompanied by twenty young, muscular, and armed warriors. The prince and his escorts were friendly, but aloof; his party mingled little with us or our slaves and porters.

For three days we traveled easily through the farms and forest Godoy had described. The young men were still at the games. On the fourth day, when we were within four miles of the capital, Soto called a halt. He sent a messenger that he and his army had arrived. The king replied that Soto could come and hold court whenever he wished.

The next morning, with the army still straggling in, Soto sent Moscoso to inform the king that he would meet with him that afternoon. Moscoso rode forward with fifteen of our best cavalry in full armed dress.

꒰

The Governor had called a halt in a small, abandoned farm village of only eight houses. There were no pyramids, temples, or a grand plaza here. Soto had settled into the largest of these thatched houses; his pages had swept it clean and set up his table and cot. It was there that he had told Moscoso that the young captain would be the first to enter the capital of Atahachi, leading a small squad of cavalry, to meet with the king and arrange for Soto's entrance.

As I knew I would wait and go with the Governor, I had made Moscoso promise me to tell me all the details of his earlier arrival so I could record them in my journal. Of course, even after I arrived there were many encounters of which I was not a part. Again, I enlisted Moscoso's aid in repeating to me what transpired during these events.

Moscoso told me how he had smiled as he selected armor from one of his watertight, cedar-lined chests as he prepared for his grand entrance to Atahachi. He was, he knew, generally considered the best dressed of Soto's captains. He relished the distinction, for he knew the Governor was a man who appreciated elegant dress. Thus Moscoso had not been concerned that his chests required two extra porters—his seventh and eighth, as two had escaped and four had died.

During the past year Moscoso had given away or sold off many of his pieces of armor. He sold them for about a third or less of their value, but they were too hot, heavy, and difficult to transport and maintain. Some pieces, like his fancy mail jacket, just were not effective against the native arrows.

He had found ready market for his armor in spite of its New World problems. The buyers knew its value and prestige in Spain— and assumed they would return to enjoy both.

He had kept his favorite, lighter, blued and embossed pieces. He would wear them tomorrow to enter Atahachi. He carefully laid out his open helmet, collar, cuirass, thigh tassets, arm defenses, and gauntlets. He had carefully polished and wrapped the pieces over the months. He and his other hand-picked cavalry members would demonstrate for the heathen king and his court the might of the Christians.

Moscoso had instructed his page to have his black stallion fed and watered and ready in the morning and fitted with his battle-harness containing dozens of tiny bells. His etched front saddle plate was to be fitted and in place, as were the carved, Moorish-style stirrups. All would be ready. He would not attempt a demonstration of the arquebus or crossbow; they would show those weapons in the days ahead, although many were no longer serviceable. Both had proved much too slow, cumbersome, and difficult to maintain for use in the guerrilla warfare of *La Florida*. However, they remained excellent tools for building fear in the natives.

Moscoso rode at the head of the column with a swell of Spanish pride. Riding at his side a half length to the rear was Soto's page-interpreter, Alonso Arias. The cavalry unit followed. Even after almost a year and a half of travel and battles in this hot and humid land, the small, proud cavalry group showed well. Five rows of three men each followed the captain and his prancing black, and the morning sun flashed off the polished metal of the men, mounts, and lances. The broad trail passed by farms and stands of chestnuts and post oaks. Under the forest canopy grew a profusion of wild grapes.

Moscoso told me later how something about the clear sky and the rustle of the men and mounts sent his thoughts back to a tournament he had attended in the Spanish coastal town of Cadiz several years before. There at a banquet following the final matches the dark eyes of a young woman had bored into him. It turned out she was the young wife of a sea captain who at the time was sailing off the coast of Africa. Moscoso had spent three days of passion with her at the captain's estate overlooking the ocean. He often wondered what had become of the torrid and turbulent Malora.

A mile from Atahachi, the young prince and his warriors and emissaries stood waiting. They would lead Moscoso and his cavalry to king Tascalusa. The final mile was through well-tended farms of maize, squash, and beans. Scattered about in the fields were chestnut, pine, and hickory trees, each ancient and singular. Old men, women, and children stood watching from the fields and houses. Near the homes grew clusters of persimmons and red sumacs. Six flute players with red striped faces and feathered headdresses preceded the slow-marching prince.

Moscoso was impressed by the discipline of the warriors following the prince. The young men, who wore no paint or feathers, walked in four neat rows and wore nothing but bleached hide loin covers. The muscular men carried their ash or hickory bows over their shoulders with arrows wedged in a side belt. Each man also carried a carved hickory war club from one to three feet in length. There was no talk in the ranks and they moved like panthers on the hunt. They were well-trained warriors. Still Moscoso felt confident and superior encased in his forty pounds of armor and riding his powerful black. He smiled as his hand found his ten-foot lance and his forty-inch Spanish hand-and-half sword. He believed he could handle the entire group in an open field.

Ahead he could see the seven-foot-high palisade that surrounded the city. Out from the sharpened staked wall was a cleared grassless area of thirty yards that also circled the city. At the sound of a conch shell trumpet, a large gate was dragged open.

Moscoso adjusted the rein controlling the Moorish bit and his black stallion started high-stepping. He had bought his still unnamed mount from a trainer in Cuba and was pleased with the animal. They passed through the gate and down a broad avenue that ran between rows of large, well-maintained houses. Ahead he could see a huge plaza, and in the distance to the right elevated above the thatched roofs of the houses were the tops of a second group of raised buildings. Standing along the avenue were small groups of mostly women and children. Unlike the streets of Seville, the avenue and the area between the buildings were free of waste and garbage. In the air was just a hint of wood smoke.

Entering the open plaza, the prince and his escort angled to the right. As Moscoso made the turn he saw ahead at one hundred yards a massive pyramid. The flat-topped, towering mound contained a large house and several outbuildings.

At the base of the facing side, a colorful mass of robed dignitaries had gathered. They were not, however, a random group but appeared to have formed a disciplined, squared human courtyard extending out from the base of the pyramid.

Ten yards from the gathering, the prince called a halt and walked alone toward the group of older men. As he approached, the front wall of men stepped aside, and for the first time Moscoso could see King Tascalusa. He was seated on two giant pillows in a small portico built off the side of the pyramid. Even seated, he appeared to be a massive man, for his torso was as tall as many of his standing court members. He wore a beautifully made white feather cloak, and on his large head was a blue Moorish-style turban-crown. To the king's right one of his retainers stood in a black and white feather robe and red-feathered headdress. This man, with a ceremonious demeanor, held a circular sunshade on a long slender pole. The deerskin sunshade was the size of a shield and painted black with a large white Maltese cross. It was held over Tascalusa's head.

Moscoso signaled Arias to ride to his side; the prince, flanked by two robed retainers, turned and walked back toward them.

"The prince," Arias said after some difficult discussion, "said that his father the king will talk to no one but the Governor, and he only wishes to know when the Governor will pay his respects."

Arias's face tightened as he studied Moscoso.

"Tell him I will speak to the king." Moscoso's voice came low and hard. He felt a surge of blood through his neck and face.

The prince pushed the air with his palms, signaling Moscoso and Arias to back off.

"Come," Moscoso said, nudging his spur into the black. They pushed roughly through between the startled prince and his retainers. With Arias riding at his side, he slowly walked the black directly toward Tascalusa. Several of the courtyard members stood, attempting to block their way, but they were pushed aside with ease. Fear was in their eyes. With the horse's nostrils not more than three feet from the king's chest, Moscoso stopped.

"Tell the king," Moscoso said, "that we come in peace and friendship." Tascalusa, with eyes the size of an oxen, glanced up at Moscoso with a look of boredom and disdain; he then sat studying the rings adorning his massive fingers.

"His Excellency and Governor," Moscoso continued, "who is the lord and ruler of all of these lands, will visit the king within the hour. Tell him further, that I and my men will now demonstrate for him and his court the power and skill of our animals."

During the translation Tascalusa continued to ignore the Spaniards by inspecting his person or the sky above with great gravity as if the visitors were not present. At all times, the sunshade was positioned over the king's head.

"Is there anything more?" Arias asked.

"No," Moscoso said, irritation in his voice. "We're going. Turn right."

•

The city of Atahachi was near present-day Montgomery, Alabama.

At this stage of the entrada things were going well; there had been no major native resistance since leaving the Apalachee in early March. De Soto's army had ample food, porters, and women. He had let it be known that he would consider establishing a colony in the spring after meeting with Francisco Maldonado.

Obviously they were disappointed that no gold or silver had been found, but de Soto planned to ship his pearls and slaves back to Cuba. He would report that he was confident that greater treasure would be found in the vast unexplored territory ahead. Hernando de Soto was an optimistic, driven man, still confident that he would find Inca-like loot in La Florida.

Chapter 15

Moscoso cantered back to where his cavalry waited and gave them their orders. After circling the plaza at a gallop, they performed a well-known jousting game where teams, with lances lowered, charged their horses past one another; they then turned their animals from side to side and sometimes feinted toward the king.

The spectacle was well executed, but the king sat seemingly unconcerned, occasionally looking on with an expression of mild contempt. As the exercise was finishing, the Governor and his party arrived at the entrance to the plaza. Moscoso promptly arranged his cavalry so as to form a corridor for Soto across the plaza toward the king.

With full shining armor and flowing plumes, the Governor rode slowly down the line of cavalry. At his side rode Juan Ortiz, wearing a splendid maroon cape. Behind them walked Cristóbal de Espindola and ten of his finest halberdiers, their long weapons polished to perfection. Moscoso rode behind Soto's guards, and he could see that the king remained seated as the Governor halted and he and Ortiz dismounted. The king retained his look of royal disdain, hardly glancing at the Spaniards as they approached.

Moscoso suppressed a desire to draw his sword and charge the haughty goliath, but the Governor appeared unconcerned. He dismounted and walked forward, took the king by the hand, and led him to a bench at the shaded side of the portico. There with Ortiz's aid they talked.

After a short time Ortiz came and told Espindola and Moscoso that the king wished to feed the Governor and his men. The Governor ordered one half of the men to eat and when finished to relieve the others. I was in the first group.

We moved to a large, open building and sat on mats as native dancers swirled about us. The dancing women reminded me of rural Spanish dancers. The food was a spicy fish stew served with large maize crackers. The black wine was similar to that we had found in Coosa.

During most of the three hours of food and entertainment, Moscoso sat across from the king. Tascalusa sat on his pillows with the sunshade always meticulously positioned above his head. Soto and Ortiz sat next to the king; Tascalusa's lead officials formed a courtyard around him with messengers regularly coming and going. Twice Moscoso's eye met those of the king; they were cold, hard, and humorless eyes, and they looked right through him.

After the festivities, Moscoso, de Espindola and his guards followed Soto as he was led by the king and his court up the broad steps of the pyramid to the palace where he would be quartered. It was a large, airy building with polished wooden floors and walls.

Moscoso stood with the Governor's guards as the Governor made a short speech thanking the king for their food and welcome. Moscoso moved slightly so that he could study the face of Tascalusa, for he knew what Soto would soon be demanding.

"Tell him," Soto said to Ortiz, "that I will need four hundred porters and one hundred women to assist us during our passage through his country."

At first the king looked as if his interpreter had not understood, and Ortiz was asked to repeat Soto's demand. Following that exchange a dark shadow covered the king's face as he stared at the Governor. He stood taller, his shoulders back, feet apart as he spit out his reply.

"I, Tascalusa, am not accustomed to serving anyone; rather all are to serve me. I am the king of this land." There was a long pause as the leaders stood with their eyes locked as if in a hand-to-hand struggle.

The Governor spoke without turning his head or moving his eyes. "Cristóbal, have your men take him into custody. Ortiz, he will remain with me until we leave his land. He can, however, communicate freely with his unarmed officials."

At first the king scoffed at such a decision, but three of the guards with their halberds held to their chests moved to each side and to his rear. Surrounded thus, and following a discussion with his leaders, he retained only four men, including his pillow carrier and the official with the sunshade. All the others were dismissed.

The following day the porters were provided, and the king promised the most desirable women would be made available ahead in a town named Mabila.

꒯

The Governor was a master of "lion and lamb" leadership, and the morning following the confinement of the king, he praised the native leader and his people for their understanding and aid and presented the king with a fine crimson Spanish cape. He also provided a horse for the monarch to ride—for he was to ride alongside us to

Mabila—although the only animal that could carry the giant was one of Soto's personal packhorses. Even with that animal the man's feet were but a few inches off the ground.

We moved out of Atahachi with the army stretching for many miles. Our trail paralleled the south side of the Alabama River, passing through a floodplain of tupelo, oak, and bald cypress. The following day we reached the town of Piachi, situated on the rim of a river gorge cutting through the white chalk soil. Soto demanded canoes to help cross the river, but the local *cacique* said that he had none. It took us two days to build rafts. Don Carlos and Moscoso suspected this was to delay us, but we were not able to locate the native canoes.

While building the rafts, two of our men wandered off for loot or women and were killed by a band of rogue Indians. The killings so infuriated Soto that he threatened to burn Tascalusa at the stake unless the killers were brought before him. Tascalusa was angered by Soto's sudden outburst, but he haughtily promised to have the killers available at Mabila. Juan Ortiz questioned some of the Atahachi porters about the killings and was asked sarcastically whether they were supposed to be the keepers of the Spaniards.

Following Soto's outburst many of the king's officials, who were still traveling with him, disappeared.

While we were in the process of successfully crossing the river, Juan de Anasco asked Soto to call a meeting of his lead officers. He, Moscoso, and others were concerned about the trustfulness of Tascalusa and his people. As with most of Soto's meetings, it was short, but he did agree to have two scouts accompany a group of Atahachi natives whom the king was sending ahead to ensure that Mabila was prepared for our arrival. I could tell that Soto did not share his captain's concern and that he believed that the scouts' report would confirm his thinking.

We moved west, leaving the river behind, and we entered a region of gently rolling hills with the higher elevations covered with stands of oak, hickory, sweet gum, and scattered pines. The lower levels were covered with tall grasses and wildflowers. The weather was pleasant, fair and cool.

On the late afternoon of the seventeenth of October we camped near a small palisaded town within a few miles of Mabila. There one of our scouts returned, reporting that many armed men had gathered at Mabila, and that the natives were reinforcing the palisades and clearing the foliage from the walls as if preparing for battle.

Soto's alarmed senior officers pressured him into a meeting at dawn the following morning. They advised him that he should not enter Mabila and should camp in an open field until more information could be gathered. Moscoso pointed out that the army was not gathered in disciplined ranks, but was spread out pillaging among several villages and farmsteads along the trail.

Soto listened to their warnings, but then as usual decided that he knew best. He said that Tascalusa had promised him a fine house inside the city and he was tired of sleeping in the open. Further, he thought it was a mistake to show any sign of weakness to the king and his warriors.

After the meeting Soto hastily ordered his vanguard and personal entourage to move on to Mabila, where he was eager to set up headquarters and housekeeping in Tascalusa's palace. This advance group included Espindola and a contingent of guards, Moscoso, Gallegos, and of course Juan Ortiz and myself. Also included was Father Castilla and several of his staff, as well as more than two dozen of Soto's personal retainers and slaves. The soldiers and porters with the key personal and religious supplies of the *entrada* marched in our dust. They were accompanied by a handful of Gallegos' cavalry.

I rode up beside Moscoso; we were riding behind Espindola and the guards and color-guards, as the broad trail passed through a grove of oaks and gums.

"What do you think, my friend?" I asked. Moscoso rolled his eyes at me and shrugged.

"Perhaps the hot summer has thinned my blood, but I feel a chill when I'm around that bastard Tascalusa—who reminds me of that other bastard, Antonico." Antonico was King Charles' huge personal guard who was famous back in Spain. "Here we are riding into his stronghold with more cooks and clerics than soldiers. Meanwhile, our army is back there wandering through the bean and maize fields looking for farm maidens to nail."

"I have faith in the Governor."

"Indeed, and so do I. The man has no fear, but in Peru his zeal ran him into the fire a time or two." Ahead I could glimpse the Governor riding next to Tascalusa, with the king's sunshade official and others in attendance.

"And he survived."

"Yes, but you can flip that coin once too often. Besides, a lot of good men were lost down there. . . . What's a day or two to get better organized?"

The trail now left the forested area and entered a broad plain of short grasses. In the distance, through the morning mist, we could see the high palisades surrounding the city of Mabila. Those of us mounted cantered forward with Soto.

•

As we have stated, the experts are still debating de Soto's exact route through the Southeast. They now believe that the city of Mabila was near the present-day city of Selma, Alabama.

De Soto had previously encountered the haughty attitude of native kings such as Tascalusa. Eight years earlier, in 1532, then-Captain de Soto had a very similar meeting with Inca king Atahualpa at Cajamarac, Peru.

Chapter 16

The wall surrounding Mabila was unique for *La Florida* and the strongest we had seen. I have wondered why, for the other features of the city were not distinctive. Heavy, fifteen-foot, thigh-thick posts were buried deep in the ground, and the rows of posts were supported crossways by cane-bound poles. The entire front and top of the palisade had then been plastered flat with a hard layer of a mix of mud and straw. Every fifty feet along the top of the wall there was a bastion capable of supporting up to ten fighting men. There were also numerous embrasures in the wall for use by archers. Two gates, east and west, provided the only entrances to the city.

Two hundred yards from the east gate Soto halted our small group of riders to study the situation and give the trailing vanguard time to close ranks. As we watched, the gate opened, revealing a group of painted natives; we could hear singing and flute playing, but the first person to come toward us was one of our scouts, a man named Xaramillo. He walked rapidly over the open ground as the native Atahachi officials organized their welcome.

"Excellency," Xaramillo said, the portly man short of breath, "is it satisfactory for me to speak freely?" Tascalusa sat on the pack horse looking awkward alongside our well-mounted Governor.

"Certainly," Soto said, "speak up." Soto did not permit Tascalusa's walking aides to slow our progress when riding in advance.

"I do not like the situation here," Xaramillo said. Sweat had beaded on his forehead. "Many armed young men have gathered in the city, and I have seen not a single old man or woman, and no children. Further, several huts and trees that were close to the outside of that wall have been torn down and carried off. And I have seen their lead men out here in this very field training young men with spears and clubs."

Moscoso nudged his horse forward so that he was alongside Soto.

"Sir," Moscoso said, "with all respect, I believe we should camp outside of the city, at least until we have the army here with us."

Soto removed his helmet and mopped his face with a blue bandana.

"I understand your concern," Soto said, his lips pulled back as his head turned to study the wall of the city, "but we must show no fear. A few of us will go in; I wish to see the situation for myself. And I plan to sleep there tonight."

The city *cacique* and his officials were moving toward us, along with entertainers playing music, dancing, and singing. The sun bathed their painted faces and feathered headdresses. The *cacique*, a large-bellied man, presented Soto with three beautiful marten skin blankets. Except for the *cacique* and three of his aides, the party was composed of younger, athletic men.

We dismounted and short welcoming speeches were made. The *cacique* said he would provide, later in the day, the women and additional porters that Tascalusa had promised. The natives seemed friendly, and we walked with them toward the gate. The music and dancing continued. Tascalusa's court had arrived and was back in attendance of their king.

We tethered our animals along the wall near the gate. The

wall looked even more formidable up close. The remainder of our advance party gathered and placed their cargo at the wall on each side of the gate. A squad of Espindola's guards and the handful of cavalry would join the regular footmen in guarding the porters with their valued cargo, as well as protecting Father Castilla and his party, the pages, and numerous other servants and tradesmen. Our advance party numbered about fifty plus, about an equal number of porters and slaves.

Soto directed Moscoso, Gallegos, Ortiz, Espindola with six of his halberdiers, and me to join him in entering the city. I walked with Moscoso and Gallegos as we followed Soto, Ortiz, Tascalusa, and the *cacique* and his officials. Several hundred additional painted and cheering natives greeted us as we walked through the gate and passed whitewashed houses with steep cane roofs. Ahead was the main plaza, but here Soto halted the procession. He told Espindola, who with his guards was bringing up the rear, to have his outside guards bring our horses inside the gate and hold them there. I can only think that for the first time Soto may have had some second thoughts as to our circumstance. Following that brief delay, we proceeded, walking through the cheering crowd to the place of honor at the head of the plaza.

Mabila was a city of some eighty houses with the largest and most important built around the plaza. Two of these houses had been set aside for Soto—one for him and one for his servants and staff. During this time I had observed nothing suspicious about the city and its cheering inhabitants, and I was questioning Xaramillo's warning.

We slowly made our way across the plaza. We were heading for a sizable thatched portico on the far side. The scene was a colorful if confusing mix of singing, dancing, and flute playing. The painted men wore only loin cloths. I saw a few young, unpainted women in the crowd. Scattered clouds had rolled in; it looked to be the beginning of a pleasant fall day.

We were ushered to the portico where I sat at a second-row table with Moscoso, Gallegos, and Espindola. The halberdiers stood at our rear. We were shortly served trays of fruits and nuts, and gourds of the popular black wine.

As we ate and drank we were entertained by teams of dancing, juggling, and flute-playing men. It was cool and pleasant in the shade of the portico. Even the cautious Moscoso relaxed. At the front table were Soto, Ortiz, Tascalusa, and other officials. At breaks in the entertainment, the two leaders engaged in conversation, and I somehow had a feeling that it was not all lighthearted.

After an hour or more of this all-male entertainment, twenty women suddenly appeared. Ten wore red loose-fitting tops and short skirts; the other ten were in similar outfits of yellow. Their faces and bodies glistened with a light film of pecan oil. Over the many years since that day, Moscoso and I have again and again reaffirmed that this was the most beautiful group of women that we have ever seen at one time together. Because of their dancing and stunts, and their loose clothing, we were able to see every gorgeous inch of their desirable bodies.

During the first part of this attention-gripping performance, I saw Tascalusa rise and leave the table. With my mind elsewhere, I gave it little thought, and for the next half-hour the women swirled, dipped, and jumped around us, and our gourds of wine emptied and were refilled.

During a performance in which two rhythmic hand clapping

women held a pole close to the ground while others remained on their feet and, with their faces to the sky, slithered under it, Juan Ortiz turned and leaned over our table.

"The Governor," Ortiz said to me, "asks that you come with me while I tell the king that the Governor wants him back here."

I strapped on my helmet and took a final sip of wine, and as I stood I caught a glimpse of the private mound of a dancer inching her way under the pole. Ortiz looked at me with raised eyebrows. It was a special performance. The painted faces of the crowd parted as we made our way through toward a large house at the edge of the plaza.

"What's this all about?" I asked as we cleared the dense pack of smiling faces.

"Tascalusa told Soto that he could travel on through his land in peace, but that he, Tascalusa, would be remaining here in Mabila. The Governor said no, he would be treated well, but he would be traveling with the army until we left his land. This, of course, did not set well with the king, and he went to talk with his principal advisers."

"What did Soto expect?" I asked. Ortiz shrugged and shook his head. We were soon at the house that Tascalusa had entered. The entrance was packed with unarmed and unpainted young men. There was no dancing and singing here, and the men appraised us with dark, scornful eyes. They made no attempt to move out of our way, and when we attempted to push through they resisted our passage. Although I was wearing my sword this certainly was no time for its use.

Ortiz spoke with a muscular man who stepped forward and appeared to be a leader. He turned and entered with Soto's message for Tascalusa.

"These aren't just farm boys," I said, as we waited, "and they're not friendly." To me the natives' eyes were hate-filled and challenging as they carefully scrutinized my armor and weapons.

"I have," Ortiz said, "told the Governor several times that I believe this show of friendship is a false act."

"What does he say?"

"That this may be the truth, but fear will control them."

We waited for ten minutes, and during this time two of the men left the group and circled around us to better see our clothing and weapons. Their faces were filled with contempt.

"What's the delay?" I asked. I knew the Governor would be getting impatient.

Ortiz talked to the two circling men, and finally one agreed to go in and tell the first messenger to come out. In a few minutes the first man came out and told us that Tascalusa was not coming out, and that Soto must leave now. If he did this he could go in peace; otherwise, Tascalusa and his allies would force him to leave.

With this ominous message we walked rapidly back to the portico. The Governor's lips tightened ever so slightly as he listened, but he said nothing. He stood strapping on his helmet, and he told Espindola to alert all the men and have a messenger ride back to speed forward the lagging army.

"Gentlemen," Soto said, his head shifting from Ortiz to me, "let us go and talk to this foolhardy king." We followed Soto as he marched across the plaza where the dancers and singers seemed unaware of any trouble. As we neared the house that Tascalusa had entered, one of Soto's personal guards came running from the direction of the front gate.

"Excellency," he was out of breath, "we have seen natives

recovering hidden weapons from palm leaves near the wall."

"Take a breath," Soto said.

"Further," he continued, straightening his helmet, "I looked into one of the houses and it was filled with men with weapons."

"Report this to Captain Gallegos and the other officers on the portico." Soto pointed in their direction and then waved Ortiz and me forward. When we reached the house there was still the cluster of men at the entrance; several of the men were now armed with clubs and maces.

Soto attempted to enter the house but was physically restrained. His eyes went stormy dark, but he made no move toward his sword.

"Tell them we wish to speak with our friend the king." A leader carrying a mace stepped forward and spoke with Ortiz.

"He says the king does not wish to speak with you."

"Tell him that he may remain here in Mabila, but we wish to speak with him and then we will leave in peace, as friends." This went on for almost an hour, but the king would not reply or come out.

Fury was building on the Governor's face and in his voice.

•

Scholars now believe that Tascalusa had been considering an ambush or attack on the Spaniards at Mabila for weeks, probably from the time de Soto first restrained him.

The dancing women at Mabila must have been beautiful, for Moscoso ended up marrying one. Her beauty became renowned throughout Mexico.

Chapter 17

"Ranjel, get Captain Gallegos over here."

I trotted back through the thinning dance crowd to the portico, and both Gallegos and Moscoso hustled back with me.

Soto immediately ordered Gallegos to go in and bring out Tascalusa. The loyal Gallegos did not hesitate; he bulled his way through five surprised warriors at the entrance with little difficulty.

Within minutes he emerged with his hand clutching his sheathed sword.

"On my mother's grave," Gallegos said, his eyes like fresh-picked chokecherries, "there are at least two hundred armed men jammed in there. They're in the rafters. They're everywhere."

"Moscoso," Soto said, his hands tightening his helmet strap, "get the word out. Have our horses brought up." Moscoso raced back toward the portico.

My eyes caught those of Juan Ortiz. His eyes were not the usual intelligent, friendly eyes; they were eyes filled with a dark fear. My hand located my sword, and a ripple of anxiety worked through me.

No sooner had Moscoso left than a native official came from a nearby house toward the entrance where we stood. He was a large, older man of Soto's age dressed in a long marten skin robe; he had traveled with us as part of the king's entourage. Gallegos stopped him, and Soto directed Ortiz to tell him that he should tell

Tascalusa that he would not have to travel with us, and if he came out and provided guides and porters we would leave in peace.

"I am not a messenger of the king's," the man replied, his head held back, eyes defiant.

"We understand, but give Tascalusa our message," Ortiz said.

"I am also not a messenger in your command," he said, spitting out the words with his bold eyes on the Governor. He then pushed his way between Ortiz and Gallegos. Gallegos grabbed the man's arm, but somehow the man, falling to one knee, slipped out of both the grasp and his robe, leaving Gallegos with only the marten skins. As the near-naked official turned to rush into the house, Gallegos slashed at him with his sword. The blow severed the man's left arm below the elbow. I can still recall the thud as the wrist and hand hit the ground.

The man went to his knees, his ashen face studying the severed hand lying in the grass before him. He was in disbelief as blood gushed from the stump like water from a punctured dike. Two young warriors rushed forward and carried him, trailing a stream of blood, into the house.

We drew our swords and moved back from the house, and within minutes, an unarmed Atahachi came to the entrance and, placing a massive conch trumpet to his lips, he blasted a long, loud call. It was a call to arms.

Within an instant, armed warriors were pouring from many of the houses around the plaza and elsewhere throughout the city. They swarmed toward the gates and wall bastions, attacking our men at the portico and those with the horses. Three of Soto's guards raced to our aid as we backed away to face the stream of warriors now coming from the entrance of the house. There was no time for thought or strategy; it was a desperate, slashing fight to survive.

They closed in around us as we slowly worked our way back toward the gate. I have often wondered how most of us survived those first minutes of the battle, for not more than twenty of us were holding off more than three thousand natives within their fortified city. Our superior weapons and armor were, without question, the major factors that October day, as was our Spanish blood. Our swords, helmets, and cotton quilted armor permitted us to form a crude circle to edge toward the gate.

The noise was deafening as the warriors charged at us. I could see hundreds on the walls cheering. Alongside a house near the wall our footmen were defending our horses.

Gallegos decapitated a man whose body careened into me, blinding me for an instant with a shower of his tepid blood. In that instant I warded off a mace to the head with my left arm, numbing it. I slashed blindly down at the mace-striking warrior. My blade hit him on the left shoulder near the head and went right through to his gut. He stood for a moment and then wilted into the grass. I wiped his entrails off my sword by passing it through his long hair.

Twice during this chaos Soto fell and we helped him to his feet. I could see arrows protruding from his quilted jacket. I had pulled arrows from my own front and knew that there were several in my back. Still, in this confined fighting, the bow and arrow was risky for the natives, for during a lull in the action I saw one native being carried off with an arrow in his chest.

Over the years I have thought how easy it would have been for the natives to overwhelm us by sheer numbers. Some would have died, but they were dying by coming at us two or three at a time. Certainly, Soto had not appreciated the cunning and power of Tascalusa in organizing his warriors, but they too were failing to capitalize on their superior numbers.

"Solis! Ranjel!" Soto shouted. "Go for the horses."

Mendez de Solis was one of Soto's personal guards. He was the army's wrestling champion, a pleasant young man from the north in León. I caught his eye and he gave me a half grin. The two of us broke off from our group, slashing our way through the disorganized mob of warriors toward our footmen defending the horses. I could see natives on the wall with their bows and arrows. Much of the way I walked with my back to Solis; his ever-threatening sword acting like the lowered horns of a charging bull. My right arm was weary, and I was gasping for air. The air hung thick, tasting of dust, blood, gut, and a mass of heated bodies.

As we approached the footmen, I could hear them cheering our progress. Then I stumbled over an unseen, slippery corpse. I went down on my left arm; a warrior dove over me swinging his mace at Solis. I heard a clang as it hit Solis's steel pauldron. My sword eviscerated the man, his insides spilling over me like a pail of squirming finger-eels. Blindly I scrambled to my feet, and in desperation I slashed out at a shadow. My razorlike blade found the side of an enemy's head, and the blade jammed in the victim's skull. It looked for an instant as if he were attempting to swallow my sword. As he fell, I needed to put my boot on his face to extricate the blade.

Solis and I stumbled through the line of footmen, both gasping for air. Our horses were tied by a house that had protected them from the archers positioned on the wall behind. These horses belonged to Ortiz and me, as well as to the Governor and the officers who had entered the city following Tascalusa.

"I'll take," I shouted to Solis, "the Governor's horse. You bring Gallegos' and Ortiz's." Solis nodded as we sheathed our swords. He seemed relieved not to have the Governor's horse. He rode well, but he did not ride often. I had a canteen on Boot and I took a couple swallows and handed it to Solis; he nodded his thanks. I could see several arrows in the back of his quilted jacket. We freed the four wide-eyed animals and mounted.

"I'll go first," I said. I was the better horseman and was comfortable with Boot.

Leading the Governor's horse, I walked Boot through the line of battling footmen, and then raised him up on his back legs. This sent the circling natives in a panic retreat. Most of these men had not seen horses before our arrival and were terrified of them. Two arrows embedded hard into my chest armor

I turned in my saddle and motioned Solis forward. He looked up and nodded.

It was his last view of his earthly life, and I can picture it clearly as I write. A bone-tipped cane arrow entered his left eye. He slumped forward and I could see the arrow protruding from the back of his head as he slid from the horse. One of the footmen scrambled onto the horse; a second man tugged on the arrow in the back of Solis's head. I turned and spurred Boot out toward the Governor.

With the natives in momentary disarray, the Governor rushed forward and I helped him into the saddle.

"Go out and get the men up here," he shouted.

He then charged his animal toward the fighting near the portico. The man had no fear. I hesitated a moment as Ortiz mounted, and he followed as I raced toward the gate. The natives were scrambling out of our way, and the gate and surrounding wall was in chaos with celebrating natives. As we advanced I saw that the porters were bringing our goods into the city and with the help of the Atahachi were striking off their chains.

At a full gallop we charged through the gate. I could see several dead horses outside the wall.

•

The Battle of Mabila is believed to be the largest single battle ever fought between Europeans and native North Americans within the continental United States. This includes battles such as that at Little Big Horn in Montana. It is estimated that over three thousand natives and fifty Spaniards died that day. The battle was part of the chain of events that led to the ultimate disintegration of this and other Native American societies in this area.

Chapter 18

It would be a day that forever altered the lives of every survivor; indeed, it changed the *entrada* itself. But once the blood flowed red, Hernando de Soto stepped to the fore. He was in his element.

Everywhere was terror and tumult. As I turned Boot back toward the city from a brief effort to urge our foraging men into action—for we still needed food and provisions, I saw the Governor come charging through the city's east gate, his head low near the neck of his galloping horse. His shoulders and back were a pincushion of arrows. He was closely followed by four cavalrymen, and a hundred yards out they were joined by Moscoso and Gallegos. Those two and a few footmen had escaped through the west gate. When the group was beyond arrow range, Soto held up his hand and brought them to a halt. I joined the assembly, and Moscoso called for all officers present to gather. Captains Anasco and Lobillo were among those assembled.

Dust swirled about us as we circled in around our leader, our mounts snorting for breath. We could see and hear native warriors pouring out through the gate; a few shot arrows harmlessly in our direction. The bodies of several of our men and horses could be seen near the wall. The top of the wall was crowded with more cheering natives. Many were waving items rifled from our cargo: weapons, flags, clothing, pieces of armor, iron pots and pans, and even a silver chalice used to carry the Lord's blood at mass.

"Moscoso!" Soto yelled. "Form a line of footmen around the city. Let not one native wretch escape." His worn horse, its mane and tail matted with burrs, slowly wheeled as he spoke. Every one of us could see his tight-chiseled face, the lips pulled back in a single taut line. I knew that face; many would die on this day. He stopped his prancing horse in front of Juan Ruiz Lobillo.

"Captain Lobillo, gather the cavalrymen in four equal squads at the compass points around the city. We will attack the walls on foot and hack our way through with axes and bars. I will lead from this location. When ready, we will attack at the sound of an arquebus. All officers will assist Captains Moscoso and Lobillo."

Soto drew his sword and waved it above his head. A page had removed the arrows from his padded jacket.

"Now let us go and show the evil Tascalusa and his heathens the strength and skill of the Christian warrior. Santiago! Santiago!"

We all drew our swords and shouted, "Santiago! Santiago!"

I helped Moscoso with arming and spacing the footmen around the city. It was high noon and more men were arriving, and junior officers were fitting them in as they arrived.

During this time the natives did not advance far from the city wall; however, there were great cheering mobs at both gates. The joyous shouting and taunting from the bastions continued. They seemed confident that victory was theirs.

With footmen circling the city, Moscoso directed me to help Anasco with his cavalry squad. The men with the best armor had dismounted and were arming themselves with axes and bars for forcing an opening in the wall. They were joined by six halberdiers from the Governor's personal guard. These men, like the cavalry, were among the best armored in the army, and Soto had divided them equally among the four attacking groups.

To our rear at the forest edge the trees stood quietly, uncaring of the turmoil at the city wall, their leaves of bright yellow and vermilion flickering in the mid-day sun. My mind flashed back to a meet I had ridden in outside of Seville. It had been fall and the leaves were similar, but this was no festive fall meet.

"Captain," one of Anasco's men said, "the Governor's squad is mounting. Should we mount?" I remained with Anasco and we could see that a portion of Soto's group was indeed mounted.

"Stay as you are," Anasco said. "My guess is it's for a run at the gate." Soto's squad had mustered in front of the east gate. A large group of warriors had gathered, and many had advanced a good distance out into the surrounding field.

As we watched, Soto and a group of about fifteen lance-carrying cavalrymen charged at the warriors. They were greeted by a hail of arrows, but they charged on. However, when they were quite close to the advancing natives they surprisingly wheeled and retreated. There were moans from some of our men.

"Ah, no, fear not," Anasco said. "I believe it is an old Soto trick. . . . Wait . . . and watch." A large section of gleeful warriors charged on after the retreating horsemen. Soto and his men had almost returned to their remaining force when they wheeled and charged back at the onrushing natives with lances low, ready. When the natives realized their mistake, it was too late, and dozens were slaughtered by the lances or trampled by the horses. The remaining natives retreated into the city, closing the gate; those on the wall fell silent.

At the blast of the arquebus, our four squads advanced through a rain of arrows and rocks, their bucklers held over their heads, axes and bars in hand. It took four advances and pullbacks to hack through the clay and the crossbars and into the log proper. It was brutal work, and not a man came back without an injury.

The only nearby water was from a small, slow creek that ran through the city. At first our exhausted men fell down and drank, but later it became dark with blood and few would drink from it.

The wall was finally breached at all locations, but advances were pushed back again and again by the huge mass of warriors inside. We were losing a few men, but they were losing dozens. Anasco suggested that we pull back and starve them out, but Soto would hear none of that. Besides, there was still the hope that Father Castilla and the others were still alive within the city.

At a meeting of key officers, Moscoso, whose chin had been gashed, suggested that we fire some of the buildings.

"We could lose our key supplies," Lobillo said, a trickle of blood running from his left ear. As Soto's head rotated between the two officers, a red film passed over his black olive eyes. The ends of his sleeves were frayed and soaked with blood.

"At each attack point give two men embers," Soto said, his voice coming from deep in his throat. "And tell them to wedge them into the first buildings. When we get the fires up, we will go in with the horses."

And so the afternoon hours churned on with attack after attack; both sides were worn and weary. At the four points where we had breached the wall, bodies lay in piles slick with blood. The native mood had changed. The jeers had gone to anguished cries, and several young women had joined the fight with the same skill and determination as that of their fallen partners. The fires spread slowly from thatched roof to thatched roof and turned each framed building into an infernal deathtrap.

With the fires going, we entered the city on horses, slashing, trampling, and lancing natives at will as we charged up and down the smoke-filled streets. The air was hot and charred. Father Castillo and his party, mostly priests and the Governor's personal staff, were discovered barricaded in a large house along the plaza. A pile of native bodies blocked the main door and additional bodies could be seen lying on the thatched roof of the building where they had tried to gain entrance. The few armed men with the Father's party had fought well. The Father and his group were led safely out of the city. Still more natives kept coming from the houses, although many, when trapped, chose to throw themselves into burning buildings rather than face the sword or lance.

Outside the wall, natives attempting an escape were run down and slaughtered like wild hogs. On this day, October 18, 1540, there were no prisoners taken—the Governor's desire for revenge superceding his need for slaves.

An enormous sun was near the trees when I left the city to help with the wounded. I was so exhausted that I was unable to put my sword in its sheath. Boot's head was down and his breathing was short and sounded like walking on gravel. I slid off and fell to the ground. I was helped to my feet by a passing soldier. The entire area and the smoldering city were bathed in a vermilion haze. Everywhere there were bodies; I stepped over them as I led Boot toward the creek.

"Ranjel, are you wounded?" It was one of Soto's pages, a sandy-haired lad named Fermin.

"No, I must water my horse." He started pulling the arrows out of my quilted coat as we walked.

"I believe there is one in your side," he said. I stopped and felt back with my hand; sure enough there was one in my right side down near the hip. Now I could feel some burning.

"What should I do?" Fermin asked.

"Pull it out." There was a jolt of pain and that was all. I was too weary to feel much. He handed me the arrow; it had a plain reed point. I dropped it to the ground and stepped on it.

"I can water your horse," he said. "The Governor has me and Pepe gathering them in a safe area. We have lost several and others are badly wounded."

I handed him the reins and patted Boot on the rump. I needed to tend to a galled spot I saw on his back near the saddle. He shook his head; his breathing was easier.

Against an orange sky, a layer of gray smoke and cinder now settled over the city. I could hear pockets of fighting still going on inside the walls. New foot soldiers had arrived and were moving in as replacements. We knew that the killing must be over before dark to declare total victory, and it would be.

The Governor had told me on at least two occasions that his worst decision in preparing for the *entrada* was hiring the surgeon Yago Juan Tabora. The bone-thin addict brought bags of dried poppy fruit with him but little else. When he trimmed your hair he often looked at you with eyes that were not focused. I was one along with a dozen soldiers who had helped Tabora with injuries during the past year. He was certainly not known as a brilliant surgeon.

Almost every one of our men had wounds like my own, but those with major injuries were being placed around bonfires that were being built. The sun went down, and the last of the Indians were slaughtered or burned to death. One warrior on the wall who could see no escape had hanged himself with his bowstring from a tree at the wall. The Atahachi had fought with great determination, but hundreds were dead and other hundreds lay dying. Many had been trapped in burning buildings. As darkness descended, the moans and cries of the wounded came from everywhere, like the sounds of mountain sheep surrounded by starving wolves. I found Tabora and three footmen bandaging the badly wounded. The bandages were made from the clothing of the dead. Two of Soto's female servants were searching among the dead for clothing to use.

"We need salve," Tabora said, his eyes wild but clear. "We have mainly arrow wounds, most in the face or exposed limbs. Also some wounds from clubs and knives. But we have nothing to apply. Even oil or lard would help."

"In North Africa we used human fat," said a gray-haired veteran named Gilberto. He turned his face to the fire and I could see flecks of gore clinging to his beard.

"That would help," Tabora said.

"I'll show you," said the grizzled veteran, looking at me. "Bring the two cook women, knives, and a pot." Thus I was quickly recruited for this unholy task. I had my own knife and got another from Tabora, and I was fortunate to find two native goat skin buckets.

"We'll go into the city," said Gilberto. "There are stacks of bodies there." He and I carried torches; the two women followed with the buckets. We walked rapidly toward the gate, passing bodies scattered in the field.

"Look for fat ones," Gilberto said, kicking at a body we passed. "You can get as much from one fat as three bony. You should have fair picking, although these are mostly fighters, not female laying hens. But they should be still warm; the fat squeezes better when it's warm. Try to harvest as little blood as possible." Groups of our men were moving in and out of the gate carrying the last of our dead and wounded. They stepped around bodies in the flickering light.

As we approached the gate, bodies lay everywhere. We followed Gilberto to the left side of the entrance, where we found many of the bodies in the main passage that had been trampled by our horses. Gripping the ankle of the corpse of an older man, Gilberto dragged it face up into an open area. The warrior had died with a lance through the chest.

"Gather around," Gilberto said, handing his torch to one of the women. Drawing his knife, he went to his knees beside the body. He cut off the bloody loin cloth and used it to wipe off the lower abdomen. It was a gruesome sight in the dancing torch light. The younger of the two women, a slave from Ocale, turned to the side, gagging.

"Get over it," Gilberto said, his voice full of scorn. The older woman looked on without emotion. She had been with the Governor since the start and had witnessed hands and noses chopped off, men burning at the stake and women eaten alive by the dogs. Her eyes were black slits in a puffy face.

With his thumb and forefinger, Gilberto outlined for us the roll of fat the man had at his midriff. "This is pretty good. If there is no roll, cut from the button toward the hip." He ran his forefinger down this possible route. "There is always some fat, but with all these bodies bypass any without a roll—since we have many to choose from."

He inspected his knife in the light. "Now," he said, turning to look at the three of us, "with a roll, you cut right down the roll, like this." He neatly cut a six-inch incision along the mid area of the roll of flesh. No blood appeared, only yellow ooze. "It is important not to cut deep; the fat is just below the skin. You don't want to get muscle or gut. Then you just work it out through the cut starting from the far edges." We watched as he squeezed out the fat and with both hands neatly scooped it into a bucket.

Gilberto got to his feet, wiping his knife and hands on his pants.

"It won't take long with three of you. When you get a bucket bring it out to Tabora. Remember, a thin cut is all you need."

•

From natives captured after the Battle of Mabila, the Spanish determined that Tascalusa had planned the attack from the very beginning. However, he and his leaders had miscalculated the great advantage that defensive armor and the horse gave the Spaniards. Most native arrows were wasted against the Spanish armor, and they did not understand the use of the pike in defending against the horse. They turned and ran, only to be easily slaughtered by the lance. Further, they believed that the palisade at Mabila was invincible. Once the walls were breached the natives were too crowded together to take advantage of their superior speed and maneuverability. They became trapped like fish in a barrel.

Chapter 19

I had just made an incision when I felt a hand on my shoulder. It was the page Alonso Arias.

"Captain Moscoso wants you to come quickly. Don Carlos is badly wounded." I scrambled to my feet, handing the knife to the older woman and motioning to the bucket.

"Fill it and return," I ordered. We had worked well together. I had done the cutting; she proved good at massaging the fat out, and the other woman had held the torch and bucket. Our second bucket of adipose was well over half full.

We walked rapidly back out of the city and toward one of several fires where the wounded were being treated. Don Carlos Enriquez had become one of my best friends during the past year. The affable young man, who was married to Soto's niece, was held in high regard throughout the *entrada*. He had become somewhat of a mediator and peacemaker within the army ranks.

"What happened?" I asked Arias.

"He was charging in near the wall when his horse took an arrow in the chest. The arrow lodged in such a manner that the animal could not make a turn, so Don Carlos reached down around the animal's neck to pull it out. In doing this he exposed an area of his neck and throat, and by ill fate a flint arrow found him thus."

Ahead I could see a group of men, some with torches, standing near the fire. A dull, sinking numbness spread through me as I realized that our friend's pleasant face might no longer grace our fire.

Moscoso saw us approach; he looked tired and his beard was matted with blood. "It's bad." He gave me a quick and unexpected hug and, taking my upper arm, led me through the small group. Father Castilla was kneeling at the side of Don Carlos, whose body was covered by a blood-stained rabbit skin robe. I kneeled beside the Father, who glanced at me and gravely nodded; his pale face looked old and thin in the torch light. Don Carlos's face was pewter-gray and his eyes closed; a section of the arrow remained in his lower throat. This was a sign that nothing could be done. My tongue was like a dry rag in my mouth. The Father took my hand and placed it on Don Carlos's hand, which felt cold and damp. I gently squeezed it and softly began rubbing it. After a time his eyes cracked open and he looked at me; all I could see was the reflection of the fire in his eyes. Then he closed them and a small smile moved his lips. After a time the Father removed my hand from Don Carlos, and I stood. I walked back, and Juan Ortiz, with teary eyes, came and hugged me; he held me for a long minute.

"Ranjel," he whispered in my ear, "can anyone tell us what this hellish day has accomplished?"

"The death of many friends and foes."

I undid Juan's arms. The Governor and Gallegos were riding up to the fire. Soto stood in his saddle, for he had earlier taken an arrow in the buttock and could not sit. It would be some time before I thought much about who was responsible for all of these deaths and the loss of supplies, for I was a loyal employee, and I admired the Governor.

An hour later, at age twenty-two and far from his home, his wife, and his child, Don Carlos Enriquez died.

৵

We remained four weeks at Mabila convalescing. Twenty-one of our men had been killed and eleven more died during the following days. We had lost twelve horses and seventy had been wounded; we had to destroy six of the wounded. We estimated that three thousand natives had died, many burned to death. We torched what was left of the city, and as many bodies as possible were burned there. Then the gates were closed; it became, in fact, a mausoleum.

For the *entrada* the loss was much more than men and animals. We had lost most of the army's baggage, clothing, and possessions, including the Governor's pearls from Cofitachequi. The priests had lost all their official clothing, ornaments, chalices, wafer moulds, wheat, and wine. It was upsetting to rely on only a dry mass and no formal Communion with our God.

The loss of the two hundred fifty pounds of pearls was devastating for the Governor, for the pearls were the only portable wealth we had found in *La Florida*. He had planned to send them to Cuba with Captain Maldonado. Now there was nothing to send but a few slaves for Isabel.

Two natives had reported that Maldonado's ships were off the coast one hundred twenty miles to the south, but with winter coming the Governor decided to turn inland to find satisfactory winter quarters. There was disagreement with this decision, but the iron will of the Governor prevailed. There were fewer objections from the leaders than the foot soldiers, for they, like the Governor, had invested most of their fortunes in the *entrada*. To return to Cuba now was to admit defeat, for even a man as powerful as Hernando de Soto could never again organize a force like this had once been. However, many of the foot soldiers were tired and saw little future in this land. They wished to return and start over in Cuba, Peru, or back in Spain. Soto knew that many might leave if they could board Maldonado's ships; they did not understand or believe as he did that only tenacious conquerors were successful. He was the iron-willed leader, and he was determined that in the end he would succeed.

Looking back now, I recognize that all had changed; nothing would ever be the same. Our once-proud army moved forward like a migrating tribe. I had been forced to take clothes from dead natives and fashion a robe; it was much like the shepherds of Extremadura wore.

We suffered a long, hard winter at a town called Chicasa. To me personally the Governor was much the same, but he no longer consulted with his captains before making decisions, and he handed out harsh punishment both for natives and Spaniards. Four natives stole some hogs and were caught; two were shot full of arrows and two had their hands cut off. In another incident, several Spaniards, because of the freezing conditions, stole skins and blankets from the natives against Soto's orders. Among those accused were Soto's page, Ribera, and his chamberlain, Fuentes. Soto ordered them all to be beheaded. Only Gallegos, asking Ortiz to mistranslate the words of the local *cacique,* saved their lives. Ortiz falsely told the Governor that the *cacique* reported that the men were innocent.

With spring approaching, we prepared to leave Chicasa and Soto ordered the local *cacique* to supply us with porters. This led to an early morning attack by the natives. We were surprised and the town was burned to the ground. We lost everything, including eleven men, fifty-seven horses, and four hundred pigs. It was two months before we could recover and move on.

ॐ

The morale of the men was low when we reached the banks of a great muddy river, known as the Mississippi. This river was larger than the Danube; its turbulent water stretched for more than a mile in width. Fortunately there was plenty of maize in the area.

The following day a beautiful fleet of two hundred galleys came up the river. They were large, well built, and aligned in battle formation. Aboard were thousands of red-painted warriors with great plumes of many-colored feathers. They held colorful shields that covered the vessels' paddlers. The *cacique* sat in the stern of the lead galley under a white canopy. We had seen nothing like this in *La Florida,* and it reminded many of our veterans of what they had seen off the Peruvian coast. We had no contact with this armada, but as we built four *piragua* rafts for crossing the river, morale improved. Perhaps Soto was right and there was Inca gold still to be found.

In mid-June we crossed the great river without incident and headed north for the major city we had heard much about from the local natives, Pacaha. Pacaha was not a city of gold, but it was well fortified and had food; we stayed there a month. Soto sent forays north, south, and west. None of the groups reported anything of promise.

Lacking a clear goal, the Governor led us toward the mountains to the west. Perhaps there was gold in those hills. We crossed the rugged mountain, but found no gold. Again, forays in all directions discovered only dry, treeless plains. The men were again restless.

It was mid-October and we turned back southeast to locate a suitable winter camp. It would be our third winter in *La Florida*.

⌁

The Governor said little, but I believe he now realized that there was little hope of finding cities of gold in this area. His plan now was to return to the Mississippi, establish a colony, and build ships. He would send the ships to Cuba with the first report from the *entrada* in over three years, and he would have Doña Isabel send back much-needed supplies. The Governor still held out hope that beyond the vast dry area to the west he would find the gold that Cabeza de Vaca had spoken of.

We spent the fierce winter of 1541–42 at a city named Utianque on the Arkansas River. Much worse than the bitter cold and the snow, however, was the sudden death of Juan Ortiz. My friend took a fever and was dead in four days; after all the years here in *La Florida* as a castaway, he had so looked forward to when he could return to Cuba and Spain. His loss was a blow to the Governor, for he had been the key to our translations and intelligence-gathering system. He was replaced by a native youth captured in Cofitachequi, but no one had Juan Ortiz's knowledge of both the Indian and Spanish cultures.

Juan's death affected me more than any I had experienced up to that point in my life, even the death of my beloved grandfather. Juan was my confidant; we had both worked closely with and admired the Governor. Yet we both disagreed with his harsh treatment of natives and at times our own men. Don Carlos had been a close friend, as was Moscoso, but they were military. Juan and I both were administrative. At times this difference was subtle but at other times huge. I have often considered writing a short biography of Juan's unique life. He was a good and caring man. The Governor spoke, as I did, and hundreds were there when we buried Juan Ortiz on a snow-covered hill overlooking the Arkansas River. For the first time I truly longed to be back in Spain.

౨

Spring finally arrived, and we trudged along the Arkansas River southeast to the Mississippi. There we found a fine spot for a colony and a weak *cacique*, but across the river was a powerful *cacique* whose war canoes showed up, demanding to know who we were and our intentions. Soto replied that he was a god and the *cacique* should visit with him. The *cacique* scoffed at this statement, saying he would accept Soto as a god if he dried up the great river. Otherwise Soto could come visit him if he wished.

During the march to the Mississippi, Soto took a fever and was unable to shake it. As tensions grew with the warrior *cacique*, Soto ordered a demonstration of *conquistador* brutality. Hundreds of native men, women, and children were slaughtered without provocation, but nothing changed the militant *cacique*. He urged us to cross the river and fight in his city. Meanwhile, Soto was growing gaunt and pale, and at times he was deranged. Finally, he took to his bed, thanking his friends for remaining loyal, saying he was ready to meet his God. His friends urged him to pick a successor. He picked Luis de Moscoso. The Governor soon went into a deep decline and finally into unconsciousness. Hernando de Soto died on May 21,

1542, at the age of forty-two. The dream had vanished.

To prevent the Indians from discovering that Soto, the "god," was dead—for, of course, gods do not die—we buried him inside the town gate, but the Indians noticed the disturbed earth. Thus, that night, we disinterred the body and rowed the decaying remains out into Mississippi. We fitted the body with sandbags and lowered it into the swirling, dark waters. It was the last of a great man who to the very end thought that he would recover and achieve fantastic success.

Moscoso proved a good, durable choice as our leader, but it took us over a year to reach Mexico. We sailed into Panuco on September 10, 1543, a ragged but thankful lot. It is remarkable that three hundred and eleven of us survived. Perhaps someday I will write of that grim and difficult voyage, but now I have not the time nor energy.

•

Ranjel had, by December of 1543, made his way back to Havana. He was the one believed to have informed Isabel of her husband's death. There he helped her with the formal inventory of de Soto's Cuban property and was given his inheritance of some eighteen thousand dollars. He returned to Mexico, where he was alcalde *(mayor) of Panuco for several years. He later retired to Mexico City, where he died in 1568. Fortunately for us, he finished this journal a few years before his death.*

Here are some other books from Pineapple Press on related topics. For a complete catalog, write to Pineapple Press, P.O. Box 3889, Sarasota, Florida 34230-3889, or call (800) 746-3275. Or visit our website at www.pineapplepress.com.

The Spanish Treasure Fleets by Timothy R. Walton. The story of the expeditions of Spanish explorers told through the history of the first American currency: pieces of eight. This book traces the rise and fall of Spain's world dominance and chronicles the developments in transportation, organization, and military technology based on competition for gold and silver. (pb)

Spanish Pathways in Florida edited by Ann L. Henderson and Gary R. Mormino. This book brings together some of the nation's leading journalists and scholars to survey five centuries of Hispanic life in Florida the state where the heritage of the epic Spanish transoceanic voyage is most visible. The peninsula of Florida was discovered in 1513 by Juan Ponce de León, who had sailed with Columbus on his second voyage in 1493. Ponce de León named the realm he discovered la Florida, the Flowery Land, and from then on it became a place crisscrossed with the pathways of the Spanish bringing their culture to this new world. (hb, pb)

Shipwrecks of Florida, Second Edition, by Steven D. Singer. This is the most comprehensive listing now available, with over 2,100 shipwrecks from the sixteenth century to the present arranged primarily by geographical sections of the state. Within sections, wrecks are arranged chronologically. Extensive and heavily illustrated appendices offer a wealth of information on topics of interest to divers and researchers. (pb)

Thirty Florida Shipwrecks by Kevin M. McCarthy. There are thousands of Florida shipwrecks. This book offers thirty of the most interesting of them. Each shipwreck story has a map pinpointing its location and a full-color illustration by renowned artist William L. Trotter. There is an extensive bibliography and a foreword by Florida state underwater archaeologist Roger Smith. (pb)

Nobody's Hero by Frank Laumer. In December of 1835, eight officers and one hundred men of the U.S. Army under the command of Brevet Major Francis Langhorne Dade set out from Fort Brooke at Tampa Bay, Florida, to march north a hundred miles to reinforce Fort King (present-day Ocala). On the sixth day, halfway to their destination, they were attacked by Seminole Indians. Only three wounded soldiers survived what came to be known as Dade's Massacre. Only two of those men managed to struggle fifty miles back to Fort Brooke. One of them, wounded in shoulder and hip, a bullet in one lung, was Pvt. Ransom Clark. This is the story of his incredible journey. (hb)

Historical Traveler's Guide to Florida, Second Edition, by Eliot Kleinberg. From Fort Pickens in the Panhandle to Fort Jefferson in the ocean 40 miles beyond Key West, historical travelers will find many adventures waiting for them in Florida. Eliot Kleinberg—whose vocation, avocation, and obsession is Florida history—has poked around the state looking for the most fascinating historic places to visit. In this new updated edition he presents 74 of his favorites—17 of them are new to this edition, and the rest have been completely updated. (pb)

Menéndez by Albert Manucy. Everyone knows of Columbus and Ponce de León, but the name of Menéndez is not as familiar. Yet Pedro Menéndez de Aviles might truly be called one of the founding fathers of America, for he was the founder of the nation's oldest city St. Augustine. This book is the first to be written about him. It is based on scholarly research, but it is not just a work for the scholar. It was written for the education and enjoyment of any reader who wants to meet this remarkable man. Manucy has dramatized historic moments so that history comes alive and we find ourselves in the midst of it. (hb, pb)

The Honor Series of naval fiction by Robert N. Macomber. Covers the life and career of American naval officer Peter Wake from 1863 to 1907. The first book in the series, *At the Edge of Honor,* won Best Historical Novel by the Florida Historical Society. The second, *Point of Honor,* won the Cook Literary Award for Best Work in Southern Fiction. The sixth, *A Different Kind of Honor,* won the Boyd Literary Award for Excellence in Military Fiction from the American Library Association.

A Land Remembered by Patrick D. Smith. This well-loved, best-selling novel tells the story of three generations of the MacIveys, a Florida family battling the hardships of the frontier, and how they rise from a dirt-poor cracker life to the wealth and standing of real estate tycoons. (hb & pb)

CPSIA information can be obtained
at www.ICGtesting.com
Printed in the USA
LVHW111145230522
719471LV00004B/130